I0623343

Black
&
White

Saturday

1

"Do you work for the government?" I asked.

"No," he answered, not looking up from his laptop. Of course that was the answer he was going to give. I silently chided myself for my stupidity.

"Would you tell me if you did?" I asked, more annoyed at myself than expecting an actual response.

The man looked up from his computer for a moment and eyed me. He had sharp features, though not unattractive. "Yes," he answered, holding my gaze for a moment longer before breaking away to continue his work.

The second of eye contact surprised me so much that for a moment I had forgotten to comprehend his response. The "yes" convinced me of the honesty behind his first answer, however. Weren't government agencies required to identify themselves?

I walked around the mostly empty room, bored by my surroundings. How I had arrived here was far more intriguing. When I had gotten off work from the local news station – yesterday, I assumed – it was nearing midnight. The parking lot attached to the station was as quiet as it always was. Everything was exactly as routine until I felt what I thought to be a bee sting on my neck. I started to swat it away, only to find a needle and a blonde woman pressing the end of it. It only took a second for the fatigue and dizziness to set in. Then I heard a "Hey!" from the adjacent parking lot, but as if through an empty paper towel tube. Unable to sustain my own weight, I had fallen to my knees, hand flying sideways into my car in a feeble attempt to stabilize myself. The shout came again and two men rushed over. One came to help me up again, but I felt drunk, working hard just to keep my eyes focused. The other man swatted at and gave chase to the woman at the end of the needle. My last thought before I blacked out completely was about how strange it was that the parking lot was so populated that time of night.

Then I woke up here, with this man – who had not been one of my protectors, to the best of my recollection – typing away on the computer. "Am I your prisoner or are you here to protect me?" I asked him, trying to understand the situation.

"Both." He didn't look up. Okay then.

I remembered something on the news once about how kidnappers treated their prisoners better if they knew their names, so I decided to try.

"My name is Anna –"

"Anna Charlotte Pitt," the man finished for me, clearly annoyed. "If you please, I'm trying to work." What was I supposed to do?

Having grown up a fan of the Sherlock Holmes novels, I decided to try to get answers from my surroundings. I had long ago concluded that the methods were largely ineffective in real life, but that didn't stop me from using them now.

First, the room. It appeared to be an empty office, save for the two metal chairs and the flimsy table to match. The walls were bare drywall with only one door, a paneled roof. Two vents on the floor, one on each side of the room, and neither large enough to fit anything bigger than a house cat. Okay. Office building by the paneling on the ceiling. We were near the core of the building, since there were no windows and office buildings were always lined with windows. Probably not the first floor, as the vents were on the floor and not the ceiling.

The table and chairs were makeshift, all folding, suggesting they had been put there in a hurry. The laptop the man typed on was a Dell. Nothing special there, more than likely. As a reporter, I spent a lot of time around video equipment, and had picked up some proficiency around computers. I was by no means "hacker" quality, though.

I turned my attention to the man. He was dressed in a collared, professional shirt, but without the jacket or tie needed to make it a suit. Slacks, black. No visible mud or scuffs on the shoes. Hands appeared uncalloused, as if he spent much of his time doing precise work instead of manual labor. The knuckles did appear to have been scarred before, though. A tan around his collar suggested he had spent some time outside. He worked in real estate, I decided. Probably even procured this building. It was a fanciful explanation, but it suited me.

Suddenly I noticed him eyeing me as I studied him. I looked somewhere – anywhere – else until I heard the keyboard resume clicking. Aware that I wasn't pacing anymore, I started moving again, hoping for another angle on the contradictory man. In the past, I'd had a knack for determining if people were telling the truth, and it seemed his answers were honest. So far, at least. How much he would reveal, though, was another question entirely.

"Can I go home soon?" I asked. Assuming today was actually the day after my most recent memory, I had no work and no particular place to be.

The only one to notice my absence would perhaps be my dog, Lucy. Even she got enough snacks and attention from the neighbors while she was in the yard, she would be set for food and content without me, save for missing her bed last night.

There was no change in the man's focus nor any suggestion he had heard my question. "Maybe I'll just kill you and walk out," I said flippantly, throwing my hands in the air.

Suddenly and silently the man stood and glided up to me, standing at least half a foot over me and glaring down. I knew immediately I would be outmatched if it came to a fight. I held his gaze and set my jaw, not wanting to show how intimidated I really felt. It was a trick I learned when people tried to intimidate me away from a story. Despite my outward appearance, my heart was racing.

After what felt like an eternity, but really couldn't have been more than ten seconds, the man blew air out his nostrils and went back to the table. To my surprise, however, he closed the laptop instead of sitting in front of it. He swept it off the table with ease and went to the door. He paused, however, with his hand on the door handle.

The strange man turned his head slightly to speak over his shoulder, but did not face me. "Stay." His voice was firm. Then he simply opened the door and walked out.

Now was my chance to escape. I assessed the room again, but even as I did, I realized a voice inside me didn't want to. What had happened last night? Why me? The little voice was growing louder with my curiosity. I was going to figure this out. I had to admit it to myself, I was a reporter, born and bred to seek the truth.

"Stay." Black had spoken with authority, but he had left to seek some. If she was smart, it wouldn't take much for the wall to fall apart if the reporter struck it with a leg of the folding chair. But Silver wasn't far from the door as Black exited and could stop her, if need be. Black needed to see the boss. And he needed to get out of that room, if he was perfectly honest with himself.

The door to the Saturday's office was slightly ajar, so Black stepped in and waited to be acknowledged. The room was dark, the only light coming from a map of the city projected on a dry erase board.

"Join us, Black," the older man invited, standing. He was in charge of the whole operation – the one they called Saturday. The founders were a group of seven, and they had addressed each other by days of the week. Three were now dead or presumed dead, including Black's brother, another departed from the organization, and another arrested, leaving only Saturday and Tuesday. The rest of the people involved under Saturday called each other by the names of colors. Tuesday's people were all types of rocks or minerals, as Black understood it. Those naming schemes had proved far less finite and far more telling than the days of the week.

His last name actually was Black, incidentally, but only a few, those who were a part of the organization before him knew that. "Where is Tuesday?" he asked after being invited into the conversation. The man ran his own division of the organization in Arizona but had spent the week nearby for a visit.

"Here," chimed in the hollow male voice over the speakerphone in the center of the room. "Any news on our friend?"

"Nothing that I could find," Black said, setting the laptop down on the conference table and plugging it in to charge. "She's a reporter, if you can go so far as to call what she does news." News in this town mostly consisted of cats stuck up trees and fundraising events. It was one of his favorite things about this place. "Her most recent story was about a comfort animal that found its way home."

"Selfies?" Saturday asked. An odd question, but it didn't take Black long to understand why he asked. If there were many, it would imply a superficial person, in which case she was likely targeted for blackmail of another person or ransom. In contrast, if there were only a few, they could assume she was the target of her own merit.

"Two," Black answered. "Both for stories."

"Family?"

"Only child. Mother died in a car crash two years ago. She doesn't seem to have spoken to her father since." Black glanced around the room. Two others were there, Green and

Scarlett. Scarlett was the only female within this branch of the organization. She had flirted with him on multiple occasions, but Black suspected she taunted him merely for the thrill, and he had never had much interest.

"Graduated in journalism two and a half years ago and signed a contract there before moving here to report. Most of the pictures she posts are of her dog or coworkers. There seems to be nothing significant about this woman."

"Then why would they be targeting her?" Saturday mused. Green, who was normally the one who focused his efforts on the opposition, shifted in his seat but did not offer an answer. It was he who provided the tip that they were targeting Anna and had been there to help protect her and bring her in last night.

"Did you ask her directly?" Tuesday asked through the box in the center of the room.

"No," Black confessed.

Saturday was quiet, letting Tuesday coordinate them even though they technically didn't answer to the Arizonian. Having served in the Air Force once upon a time, Black had to continuously remind himself that civilians paid far less attention to rank and file than his mind wanted to.

"Good. Let her go," Tuesday instructed, "but keep an eye on her. They might show themselves again. So long as she knows nothing, she can't harm us. We'll get more if we can capture her attacker."

"Black, you and Cyan bring her back to her car," Saturday spoke up finally. Black would obey, but only because Saturday agreed. He didn't answer to Tuesday.

Aware he had been given orders, Black nodded and exited the room, leaving the laptop behind.

I sat in the back seat of the car in an uncomfortable silence. The man had put a bag over my head and told me not to remove it until he said so. I obeyed, aware of little more than the fact I had been brought through an elevator, outside the building, and guided into a car.

"Okay," a different man's voice instructed after about ten minutes. "You can take it off."

I gladly reached for it and pulled. Fresh air was welcomed in contrast to my stifled breathing in the bag, and I looked around. We were near the downtown area and could have come from near anywhere in the city. My driver, on the other hand, was vaguely familiar. Where did I know him from? Had I interviewed him for something before?

"Where are you taking me?" I asked, hoping to glean more information.

"Your car is at the news station," the man driving said. Ah! He was one of the people I had seen the night previous when I got off work.

"That's it?" I asked.

"Until we know why they were targeting you, yeah."

"Who are 'we' and 'they'?"

"'They' are the government."

I bristled at the comment. "The government is on our side. Of the people, by the people, for the people." I knew several cops, something that proved helpful in my line of work, and they were all good people.

"Locally, I'd agree," my driver said. "Not nationally."

Feds? Why on earth would they be after me? And why not arrest me straight out for whatever the cause was? Then the law could sort it out. The law rarely failed, in my experience.

"What's your name?" I asked, curious. If I figured anything out, I would be interested in contacting him for an interview. This one was much more conversational and nicer than the one on the laptop earlier.

The man hesitated only a moment before answering. "Cyan."

"Is that your real name?" I asked, skeptical. This whole cloak and dagger routine was getting old.

The driver turned the wheel, taking the off-ramp toward the station. "No." Fair enough. I waited for the light to turn green before he pulled into the parking lot. As Cyan, if he wanted to be called that, slowed the car to a stop, he grabbed a bag from the foot area of the passenger seat. "There you go," he said, handing it to me. It contained my purse, keys, and phone. All the things that had disappeared at the time of my abduction.

"Uh, thanks." I put everything back in their respective pockets.

"Off you go," he insisted, though gently.

The moment I stepped out of the surprisingly expensive-looking car, Cyan sped off, the sudden speed closing my door before I could. I went to my own VW Bug and paused. I could verify this man's story right now. We had a digital archive of all the press releases – I could see if my name was wanted on any of them.

I stared into the planter next to my parking spot as I thought. The sod had been disturbed and a branch of a bush was smashed. It looked like a crime scene, but without the tape. Why not double check?

"Are you on call this weekend?" Matt, the weekend producer, asked as I walked in.

"Nah," I responded, not eager to volunteer to help. Suddenly I realized I had nixed my reason for being there at all. "My, uh, camera battery died. Is Suzanne here? I've an idea for a story." If there was actually some sort of government conspiracy, I was the perfect person to blow this wide open.

"I think she's in her office with Jenny right now."

"I'll wait, then." I sat down at my computer where I had a clear line of sight to Suzanne's office. I opened the network folder that held digital copies of any press releases faxed to us. There were several that had come in after I had last read through them, but none even held a name I recognized, besides the officers involved.

So Cyan, and his whole organization, whoever they were, were wrong. I rubbed my neck and stretched, realizing too late I had pressed on the tiny bruise where the needle had gone in. Was it a case of mistaken identity? Possible, I supposed, but unlikely. I had a pretty public face in this town, especially since I was the only dark-haired female reporter at the station.

The door to Suzanne's office opened and Jenny stepped out, writing a note on her tablet. I was four steps away from my desk before I realized the warrant database was still open on my desktop. I sprang back, clicked the little x in the corner, and rushed to the boss's office.

I had been in this room a hundred times, at least, in my past six months here. My inner child still felt like I was in the principal's office every time, despite the fact that Suzanne was one of the best and most caring bosses I could ask for.

"Anna! Have a seat." Suzanne clicked her mouse a few times before turning her attention toward me. "How's it going?"

"Going well," I answered. Part of me felt like I should be panicked after yesterday's ordeal, but I really wasn't. More like curious. "A story has just fallen in my lap. How hard would it be for me to take the week off to pursue it?"

"A week? What's the story?" Most days I was assigned two stories; one if it was a big deal. Suzanne's surprise at my timeline was understandable, now that I thought about it. I just wanted to do this right, if it turned out to be anything at all.

"I'm not sure yet. Could be nothing. I'd come back in after I know it's concluded."

"I don't see why not. We're at full staff this week, so we could spare you. You'd have to use the time to work, and if it doesn't pan out, then apply vacation time afterward. Fair enough? You do have a week's worth of vacation, right?"

"Yes, thanks." I stood, eager to leave before she could rescind her approval.

"Oh, and Anna?" I turned and smiled, despite my inner dread that she might change her mind.

"Yeah?"

"Keep track of how much time you spend on this. If it turns out to be worth a week of your time, HR will need exact numbers." Right.

"Will do. Thanks!" I grabbed my camera from my desk and left before a disaster broke out.

2

Cyan had dropped Anna off, so now it was Black's turn to watch her. From his view in his van, he could see both the front and back of the news station. If she left, he'd know. Recordings of Russian language classes played as Black watched, helping keep him from being bored. Surveillance was by far the most tedious part of his job.

Not that he was paid to be part of this. None of them were. But as a retired military officer, money wasn't a big deal in Black's life. He had no family to eat out with or purchase gifts for. His brother was out of the picture now. So Black's money went to gas and housing. And recordings of foreign language lessons.

Black watched as Anna left the building and got into her car without incident. It wasn't likely that they would attack again right away, but he had to keep an eye on her until they did.

It wasn't hard to follow her home. She was a good driver, keeping lots of space in front of her and using her turn signals. The suburb she lived in held two apartment complexes, one at each end. Black followed her to the second one and parked the van across the street, leaving the engine, and therefore the AC, running just a little longer.

As Anna got out of her car, she looked around, eyes resting on Black's side of the street. For a moment, he thought she had made him, but she closed her car door and proceeded to her second story apartment regardless, camera slung over her shoulder.

An hour wasted away, then two. Black found himself pondering the situation – pondering Anna – and several times skipped back on his recordings after being lost in thought. She was quick and intelligent, that much was certain. Maybe a little careless, in Black's opinion, but then again, most people were. Twice an hour, Black walked around the block, keeping an eye on the apartment complex the entire way, and remembering to change his appearance every time in case nosy neighbors got suspicious. Jacket and messy hair one time, rolled up sleeves and tennis shoes the next.

The fifth time around he noticed something. A new car, on Anna's side of the street, driver waiting inside. Could be nothing, but Black slowed his jog and pulled his headphones out of his ears anyway. The man in the car set a file aside on the passenger seat and got out. Black leaned over, as if out of breath, and watched. CA EXEMPT on the license plates. Government vehicle, then. The man approached the stairs closest to Anna's apartment and climbed. Boyfriend? Black didn't think so. Her Facebook account showed no indication of a significant other.

Black stretched slowly and started aiming to go across the street, jogging in place as he waited for traffic to pass. The mysterious man tried the front door to Anna's apartment as Black jogged across and, finding it unlocked, went right in.

Time to run.

It didn't take more than another twenty seconds for Black to get to the front door, which had been left open.

Black knocked. If the man was here with violent intentions, then it would be better that he targeted Black than Anna. Water was running in another room, likely the bathroom.

A quick survey of the front room revealed it to be empty of anything significant. TV was left in place, so that confirmed this wasn't a run-of-the-mill robbery. They were after Anna. Turning right, Black caught a sight that made even his military-hardened stomach turn.

There, in the kitchen, was a dog bleeding out on the tile. Lab, by the looks of it. Fully grown, it was on its side, chest heaving with the struggle. It glanced up at Black before closing its eyes. A twitch of the back paws could have convinced him that the animal was asleep, chasing rabbits in a dream, before the struggle stopped entirely.

Black didn't want to look anymore, so he turned and began his search. A standing wall separated the front door from the bathroom, with two options to lead him there. Left, he decided. The living room. If the government's man escaped behind Black out the only door to the apartment, then he'd be forced to go through the pool of blood in the kitchen and at least leave tracks.

A scream split the silence. Like a shot from a starter pistol in a foot race, the sound was all Black needed to get moving at full speed. The layout of the apartment was simple, and in no time at all, he found them in the restroom. The man held a gun up toward Anna, who was in the shower, hair still foamy from soap and water still running. Black grabbed the closest thing, a hand towel on the sink, and flung it in the man's face as he turned to face him. Black waved his left hand to counter the gun swinging toward him. A shot rang out, far from hitting any target, but remarkably loud in the small room even with the silencer. With his right hand, Black brought his knuckles down on the bridge of the man's nose, simple as knocking on a door.

In his shock, the man loosened the grip on the gun but unfortunately he did not drop it. As Black was wrestling for the weapon, the man stepped forward and punched Black's kidney. Pain splashed Black's insides, but he managed to keep his focus. Instead he clamped his left hand around his opponent's extended arm, the one with the gun at the end.

It didn't take more than a twist to pop the man up on his toes, creating a gap under the extended arm for Black to go through. For a brief moment, they looked like school children playing London Bridge before Black was on the other side, contorting the arm he still held until the man's choices were to drop the gun or get his arm broken behind his own back. They stood for a moment, both facing the door Black had entered through with Anna safely behind them.

"Come on," Black said absently, the same way he spoke to a computer as it processed. "Drop the gun." He twisted up, putting the man in front of him on his toes again. Black heard and felt rather than saw the gun leave the man's grip and clatter to the floor. Satisfied, he knocked his head against the back of the other man's and pushed, sending him face first into the bathroom floor, Black almost riding him as he fell.

"I give!" came the shout from the face turned against the cold tile. Keeping a knee on the small of the man's back and his right hand holding the man's arm, Black reached back for the gun. Grasping it by the muzzle, it took very little effort to pistol whip him and knock him out cold.

Black stood, tucking the gun into his belt, and pulled a towel off the rack on the wall, offering it to Anna. Her eyes were still locked on the man on the floor for a moment. Then they snapped back to Black and he watched her recognize that she was naked, shower still spewing over her. She snatched the towel before wrapping it around herself and turning off the water. Black let her have her privacy, instead patting down the unconscious man on the floor. Two blades, one three inches and the other around six. The larger had a partial serration on it and what Black assumed to be dog blood.

Then he found what he sought: Zip ties. He wrested the man's left arm back behind his back and zipped the wrists together. It wouldn't be inefficient to use another, this time perpendicular to the first and between the wrists. The resulting knot of brittle plastic secured Black's prey. Without being able to see the ties, it would be very difficult to understand and therefore escape on his own.

Black felt Anna brush past him and out the door as he took his time tying the shoelaces at the top eyelets on the man's boots together. Both boots would have to come off together – something else the man couldn't do without help so long as his hands remained tied – in order for him to walk or run.

My camera. I had figured it out before the men had burst into my shower. It was the only logical reason why they would be after me. I must have captured something of value to them. What, I had no clue. I scrambled into jeans and a t-shirt – not my normal everyday wear, but a fashionable dress and heels made no sense in light of the circumstances. I reached for my gym shoes and froze. My hand was shaking violently, unbidden. Stop it, stop it, stop it! I clenched my fist and flexed it open again, but that only helped a little. I grabbed the shoes anyway and tried to ignore it.

Suddenly I realized I hadn't seen my dog. "Lucy!" I called, trying to keep the panic out of my voice for her sake. "Lucy! Come here, girl!" I listened for a moment, but didn't hear her running to me. "LUCY!" I shouted this time, openly panicking. Then I heard sounds coming toward me, but they were far too heavy to be her.

The man who had fought my attacker minutes ago showed his face again. "Shut up!" he snapped.

I didn't care. "Where's my dog?"

"Dead." The man turned to leave. I could only stare at his back as I began to comprehend what he said. Dead? She couldn't be! Lucy was my mom's dog before she died, and all I had taken with me when I moved out here.

The shaking in my hand was back, and fiercer than before. I stood, gripping my shoes in one hand and my bed in the other as I rose. "Where is she?" I asked, following him as he searched my place.

"I told you, dead," he responded, looking around the living room, then pulling a knife and reaching for the couch.

"I heard you. But I have to see her."

"Behind you, in the kitchen."

I spun, and instantly regretted it. The sight made my stomach boil. There she was, on her side, almost appearing asleep in a bed of her own blood. The only indicator otherwise was the gash across Lucy's neck, pulled wide to reveal the flesh underneath the fur.

I couldn't hold it any longer: I threw up. I managed to hold the contents in my mouth as I lunged at the sink. Sour and liquid, my stomach emptied itself inches away from my fruit bowl. The last time I had eaten was at dinner the night previous, so basically the only stuff to come up was stomach acid and chunks of spaghetti noodles. When there was nothing left, my stomach tried twice more, to no avail. I rested my head on the cool rim of the sink and turned the water on. I spat, trying to purge the sour flavor from the back of my mouth.

This was not how I wanted to remember Lucy. I wished fervently to forget the sight, but the image seemed burned into the back of my eyelids. I tried to instead recall her playing, hiding in her favorite spot in the yard or anything else. What kind of monster would do this to her? She probably ran to him expecting a treat, but not this. Never this.

"Do you have duct tape?" came the stranger's voice in the other room. That brought me back. I opened my eyes and stared at the kitchen cabinets, not daring to look down.

"Go away."

Footsteps came closer to me. He entered my field of vision, turning the sink off. "Anna," he addressed me, gripping me firmly by my shoulders and forcing me to stand. I knew by the look in his eye that he secretly mourned Lucy too, though he had never met her. But he was clearly hiding the emotions. He felt half as awful as I did, which as much as shouted to me that he couldn't have been the one to have done that to her. I could trust this man - he was here to protect me. "Look at me. The man in your bathroom wanted to do that," he gestured toward Lucy, "to you. And I need to know why. Get over it."

   Get over it. Probably not Black's best choice of words. But he was here because he was good at finding and fighting people, not comforting them.

   The words seemed to have the desired effect, however, and she turned back toward the pantry door and pulled out a half-used roll of duct tape. It would do. The man would be waking up any minute and Black needed to prevent him from making noise. Black felt Anna follow him as he went back into her restroom.

   "Flip him over," Black ordered as he stepped past the man to manipulate him by his feet. Anna obeyed, hoisting him by the shoulders.

   "What are you going to do to him?" she asked, spitting out a stray chunk of hair that had made its way into her mouth. Black didn't know how much to reveal, so he repeated his earlier words.

   "Get him to tell me why he's here." After a quick glance, Black spotted what he was looking for: the hand towel he had used minutes ago when fighting the man. He snatched it up and stepped forward, kneeling over the man and straddling him in case he woke up. First the towel in the mouth, then the duct tape to cover it. Only about a quarter of the towel fit in, but that would suffice. Black wrapped the tape all the way around the head several times before tearing it off.

   He quickly decided she would take the heavy end, just in case the man woke up and started trying to kick. He'd rather be the target than her. "One arm under each armpit, then hoist," Black instructed. He stepped up and back, grabbing the man by the knees.

Together they managed to drag the muscular agent to the couch Black had prepared earlier. The cushions were still off, revealing the hole carved inside, large enough to carry the man but small enough to maintain the furniture's structure.

"Get your shoes on." The next step was getting the couch downstairs and into the van. While Anna did as she was bidden, Black found a throw blanket and draped it over the dog. If Anna broke again when they carried the couch out the door, it could mean trouble. Blood was already beginning to stain the outline of the blanket, but it was the best he could do at the moment.

Everything went better than expected as they manipulated the extra heavy couch out the front door. They heaved and scooched it as far as they could, but there was no easy way to proceed once they reached the stairs.

"Hey Anna! You're not moving out already, are you?"

Black immediately straightened at the new voice, ready to defend the reporter again. The voice came from a neighbor, two doors down. He had to be in his early twenties, if Black judged correctly, probably a bodybuilder with too much time to spare.

"She's just getting rid of the old couch." Black offered a hand to the neighbor as he approached. "My name's Michael." It wasn't, it was just the name Black preferred to his own.

"Me too!" The smiling neighbor clapped both hands around Black's offered one and shook. "Need some help?"

"That would be great. The thing's heavier than it looks."

"Really? Dan, get out here!"

Black stared as not one, but two more guys came running out. If something went awry, this could get out of hand very quickly. He sized them up as they trotted over. Michael first. Then if one still had the courage to stick around, it'd be that one versus Black.

"You guys are helping us move this thing," Michael announced. Not as an order, but in a brotherly friendship kind of way.

"Sure."

"Anything for Anna."

Anna stepped back and Black and the three young men managed to get it down the stairs and across the street. The couch tipped dangerously close to revealing its contents as it went into the back of the van, but otherwise the travel went without incident.

Anna thanked her neighbors and waited for them to be out of earshot before addressing Black. He let her take the lead, since it was clear she had something to say as he closed and locked the back and side doors of the van.

Black kept his eyes on the van as Anna spoke. "I'm going to go back and get my camera. You cannot leave until I come back."

"Cameras aren't allowed – "

"I don't care." Anna's vehemence surprised him. "You conned my neighbors into helping you move a body. You owe me."

"He's not dead." He'd better not be. He'd be of no use to Black or the organization if he was dead.

Anna leveled a gaze at him. She clearly wasn't going to take no for an answer.

"Get your camera. But it only turns on if I say you can turn it on."

Satisfied, Black watched Anna jog back to her apartment before getting into the driver's seat.

3

I managed to convince my rescuer of two things during a short drive. First, he told me his name was not Michael, as he had told my neighbors, but asked me to address him as Black. I had inquired further as to the nature of the code names – all colors as it would seem – but he told me to leave it there, so I did. The man was short on words, to be sure, and I didn't want to antagonize him and get him to close up.

The second accomplishment showed an abnormal amount of trust in me. I asked that he didn't put a bag over my head, as they had last time, and he agreed. Therefore, I was able to know exactly where we were headed: a four-story office building under construction downtown. I had guessed the nature of the structure correctly that morning. I assumed the trust was because I had not revealed his true self to my neighbors. Regardless, I was grateful.

In silence we ascended in an elevator of the building, which was skeletal in a way known only to burned structures or ones being built. The moment the doors opened, Black addressed the white-haired man who stood on the other side without salutation.

"Where is Green?"

"With Saturday again, I think." Saturday? Sounded like another code name, but it didn't fit the theme.

Black started in one direction and stopped when I moved to follow him. "And Cyan?" At first I thought he was asking me because he searched my eyes as he spoke.

Fortunately, the elevator man responded. "Due back any minute."

"Good. She stays with you."

"Wait!" I protested. I moved to follow Black again. I had questions!

"No." Black spun back around and continued briskly on his path.

That single word stopped me in my tracks. Maybe we weren't learning to trust one another after all.

"Ah. You must be Anna. Everyone's a-flutter about you. Don't worry about Black. He's always like that." I turned back to the man at the elevator as he spoke, really looking at him for the first time. He was maybe twice my age and had an easy air about him.

"How do you know who I am?" I asked, alarmed at his statement.

"Because the other guys are after you. We don't know more than that. That's why we sent our best man to keep an eye on you. I didn't realize he'd bring you here, though."

"Black is your best man?" Maybe this older gentleman in front of me would be willing to divulge the answers I sought.

"For that kind of thing, yeah. We have many people with special skills, but he's unique that way."

"What is your purpose here?" I asked, finding a folding chair and sitting on it. I crossed my legs habitually before remembering I was in jeans instead of my usual skirt.

"Me? I watch the elevator. And repair equipment, occasionally. But mostly keep track of who comes in and goes out."

"So you're like a guard."

"Not exactly," the older man said, shifting his weight so he could lean against the wall. "I don't fight if something goes awry. There are younger men here for that." The elevator descended with a tone. "Ah. Cyan must be here."

"Do you know where I can find a computer?" I asked, fingering the chip from my camera in my pocket.

"You'd have to talk to Limey about that."

"Limey?" I smiled at the name. "Please tell me he's British?"

The man smiled and nodded. "That he is. Though he's an American citizen now."

The elevator rang again and the doors opened. Cyan was speaking before he even stepped out. "Hi ho Silver! Has Black —" He was mid-sentence as he crossed the threshold and he noticed me. The old man must be Silver, then. Either that or Cyan was a fan of the Lone Ranger.

"Black is talking with Green and Saturday," Silver answered Cyan's unfinished question. "Why don't you take Miss Anna here to visit Limey? She needs to use a computer, apparently."

Cyan beckoned me down the hall opposite from the one Black had gone down. As we walked, I explained my theory that whatever "they" were after was possibly something I had filmed while out on a story. Cyan didn't shy from my idea, fortunately. Together we, and Limey, spent much of the rest of the day sifting through the footage. I confess I had not purged the hard drive and formatted the chip for several weeks, so there was maybe sixty hours to go through.

Noah sat in the newsroom alone. He was on call during the afternoon and figured he would stay at the station during his shift and post some articles on the website. Near constant sound filled the otherwise empty room, coming from two sources. On the far end of the room, the early afternoon network shows played, reminding him of the current broadcast. Much nearer him, however, were the police scanners. Occasionally they played tones, and static from the conversations over it fluttered back and forth every thirty minutes or so.

Noah perused the unfinished and unpublished articles on the site. The routine was for the reporter to write the story and then leave it for another pair of eyes to check. They were supposed to be approved by the end of the day and published before they left. It was generally agreed across the reporters not to share their routine with the higher-ups. Noah took the time now to collectively cover all the reporters' tracks, so to speak.

The most recent one on the list was Anna's. Noah glanced over the story – this one about a fire – and found no errors, but there were some numbers that could have changed. Seeing no press releases since the end of her shift, at least none that pertained to that fire, Noah decided to call her, just to double-check before approving the article.

The phone only rang once before Anna answered. There was some machine hum and at least two people chatting in the distance, quickly blotted out by Anna's voice. "Hey Noah. What's up?" The hum died and he heard a click somewhere in the background as a door closed.

"Hi. Sorry to interrupt you."

"It's no problem. I needed a break anyway."

"Good. I just wanted to check that your numbers were still good. On the wildfire article last night?" Noah spoke quickly, not wanting to waste time and bother her.

"They should be. I updated them just before I left. No new press releases?" It was then that he heard a click as someone came through the front door of the station. That was odd. Early afternoon meant no one was supposed to be around for a couple of hours still.

"Huh? Oh, yeah," Noah answered, remembering that she had asked a question. "Yeah, no news on that front."

"You could go through and add viewer photos if you get bored. I didn't look at those yet." Anna's voice sounded distant over the phone. They were both distracted now. But Noah got the answer he had called about.

"I'm sure I will. Thanks!"

"See ya," Anna responded, catching that he meant to conclude the phone call.

"See ya," Noah echoed, before hanging up. He stood to get a better angle on the doorway, but the foyer looked empty, as normal. Maybe he had misheard something past the scanners and the TV.

Noah published Anna's article and moved on. The next story didn't have a video attached. He would have to dig it up in the archives to get it. Some city council meeting. He opened the network drive on his computer and went into the archives, looking for the video from last week. He clicked on the second-to-last file to open it. It took longer than he cared to admit to realize he had gone back two weeks instead of just one. As soon as he recognized this, he backed out and eyed the week dates more carefully. Last week was missing!

It didn't take Noah long to jot a note to the engineer and find tape to attach it to his door. As soon as he approached, Noah noticed movement inside. Maybe it was one of the engineers that had come in a moment ago?

"Les?" Noah called, opening the door and flicking the light on to let him know that he was there. "There's a problem with the archives."

"I'll be out in a minute!" came the voice from the other side. That wasn't Les. The voice was one of a strong young man, the opposite of their chief engineer. Maybe someone from corporate? What would they be doing messing around in the engineer's office at this hour? Noah went deeper into the room filled to the ceiling with equipment racks.

"I'm sorry," Noah said after spotting the man. He tried, and knowingly failed, to hide the alarm in his voice with politeness. "What was your name again?"

"I'm Ken." The man reached down into his equipment bag, presumably to produce some sort of ID. Smoothly, so that Noah didn't register right away what the man pulled out, Ken turned a gun on him. Extra long barrel — that meant silencer.

Ffft. Ffft.

Pain slashed through Noah's torso. The force of the bullets pushed him to the ground, on his back. Ken, as he called himself, casually walked back into Noah's view after he landed face up. All Noah could do was cough as the barrel was aimed right between his eyes.

Ffft.

"We could just carve him up and donate his organs," Black commented as he watched Green. He leaned casually against the corner of the interrogation room, with the man he had captured strapped to a chair in the center. The man was awake now, and burning a fair amount of calories in visible panic at the unexpected situation. Green, as the expert on the government's malicious activities, had the honor of interrogating the captive. Green's Army Ranger training made his mere presence intimidating, more so as he circled their captive hungrily. It made Black glad he was on their side.

"Blue wants him first," Green responded, still circling. Blue was on the local police force and could make sure this man faced the judge for all his crimes.

The man spun in his chair, keeping his eyes on Green as best he could. Fear was written on this man's face, plain as day, but so far he had said nothing.

"Who do you work for?" Green asked, pausing directly behind the man, making him turn back and forth wildly, trying to keep track of his interrogators.

Black watched the scene with a kind of detachedness. They had been there for hours. He had watched from the shadows as Green did his work, only offering a comment or two on occasion. Green had stepped out more than once, presumably to establish some unknown fears in their captive's imagination. The brief reprise meant it would be Black's turn to offer the man water.

The prisoner was skeptical at first, but it only took Black drinking it too for him to accept. Again and again Black gave the man liquid, and it was at any moment now that their captive would need to use the restroom. This wouldn't help the man confess directly, but Black knew from experience that it was far easier to maintain a stoic silence when the body had no base urges. This man's need would chip at his resolve and hopefully bring them answers sooner.

Finally he spoke up. "I'll kill you. Both of you." Black straightened, interest renewed. "It was just supposed to be the reporter, but I'll get you all."

"From there?" Black snorted, watching the man from his corner.

"Untie me and I'll prove it."

"That battle has already been fought," Green sneered, continuously pacing. "You ended up here. Tell me, do you work for the government?"

All threats ceased and the man's jaw clenched shut again.

Black pondered the question. They already knew he worked for the government. The equipment he had on him was the same as the Secret Service, minus the communication piece. He had paramilitary grunt written all over him. Even the car he had driven to Anna's apartment had government plates. They had spent their time putting pressure on the dam. Convincing him to tell them what they already knew would be the first crack that would make that dam burst.

"Say it."

The man shook his head. Black considered that confirmation enough, but he still needed to speak it.

"We already know you do," Black chimed in from the corner.

"Say it." It was an order, as if Green were pulling rank.

"What's the use in keeping it from us if we already know?" Black enjoyed, to a certain extent, working with Green for this very reason. They tag-teamed together easily and well. They had even sparred on occasion, when bored. Green was a pleasure to fight against and with.

"Say it."

Green stopped behind the chair again, and just for a moment, the silence and sudden stillness was stifling, even from Black's corner. Perspiration was obvious on the man's brow; his stress levels were high. Any moment now.

"Alright!" The man seated in the room finally broke. "Yes, yes, I work for the government." The man hung his head, chest heaving, defeated. Green glanced up at Black and for a moment they shared a smile. A second later Green was on the prowl once more.

"I didn't hear you," Green said. Black knew it was a lie; the room was silent, save for Green's footsteps and the heavy breathing of the man. They just needed him to say it again. It took a minimum of two twists of a screw before you could trust it.

"I work for the government and for Senator Lewitt." Black raised an eyebrow. The man had volunteered new information without asking? A shared look with Green told Black he didn't trust him either.

"I don't believe you," Green said, always pacing.

"Can I break his hand?" Black asked without moving, knowing he wouldn't have to.

The man was near panic now. "I swear! I used to work for Barner until I got this job under Lewitt. I get my orders from his assistant. That's all I know. It's just a job, I swear. Please."

"Why were you after the reporter?" Green circled.

"She filmed something. A story. My orders were to kill her and get all of her equipment back to them."

Green looked at Black, out of sight of their prisoner, in confusion. Black had to confess, he was just as vexed. He had watched through every story and read every article she had published in the last month, and had found nothing.

"Which story?"

"I don't know, I don't know."

"How can you not know?" Green roared. Black had to admit, the Army man was extremely intimidating when he wanted to be.

"Kill the reporter. Get the equipment. That's all."

Satisfied, and with no more questions to ask, Black opened the door and slipped out. Scarlett awaited on the other side, looking at a timer on her phone.

"Four hours and twenty-eight minutes. That's a new record, I think." She sat, sensuous and sassy as ever. "You two are getting good." Black only huffed at her nonsense, annoyed. Scarlett's posture was inviting him to stay with her, but it only summoned feelings of irritation in him. He turned away and set out to find Blue.

The officer was on patrol, as it turned out, and Silver had no problem reminding Black that some of the people here had jobs. He was joking, of course. Both he and Black were retired, though from very different careers.

"Is anyone in the spare room?" Black asked. That room had a cot, among other simple amenities. Black had been up since well before dawn and now the sun was setting.

"The reporter. Anna." Black couldn't help but bristle as he thought that someone, who was not one of them, was sleeping there. Then again, it wasn't like she was about to go home. She would probably be spending the night here for some time. At least until Orange got to do his thing.

"I'll be at my home if anybody needs me." Black's "home" served more as an address and convenient place to stash things than a cozy cottage.

"Wait! Black!" He recognized the voice immediately as belonging to the reporter. "If you're going out, can you take me to my car?"

Black nodded begrudgingly, though he had nothing else in particular to do at the moment. Giving Anna her car back would at least get her out of his short-cropped hair.

Back at my apartment complex, I didn't dare go inside. Instead I thanked Black as I hopped out and went straight to my car. Evening was approaching, but my nap had refreshed me some and I was wide awake again, though hungry.

This area had a distinct smell around evening, probably because of the sprinkler system cycle. Fresh cut grass and water on the pavement made the area feel like home, at least as close to one as I could get. After getting my car, the next priority was food. I had the pizza place on speed dial, and they must have recognized my phone number before picking up.

"Good evening, Anna," said the voice on the other side. His name was Steve, I was pretty sure. "Your usual?" A personal pizza delivered to my apartment.

"Not today," I answered. "Two larges, one pepperoni, one combination. I'll be picking it up."

"Really? Having a party today?"

I fumbled with my keys as I sat in my car. "Something like that."

"Cool. We'll have it ready for you in twenty minutes or so."

"I'll be there in ten!"

It didn't take me long to decide to get a couple of two liter sodas to go with the pizzas and arrive back at the empty office building. Silver greeted me and stole a slice as I headed in. The whole operation didn't feel that different from the newsroom, especially when I heard an "I smell pizza?" from Cyan on the far side as I entered. Both of the men who had helped me all afternoon came over and pulled slices out of the boxes.

"I'm glad you're here," Limey said. The man had a healthy British accent that inevitably made me smile. Something about that dialect always gave me the chills in the same way my favorite song did the first time I heard it.

"Find something?" I asked, shaking my momentary distraction.

"Maybe." Limey was busy typing again.

Cyan balanced a slice of pizza with his pinkie before answering her. "We heard from Green that this whole thing might have to do with Senator Lewitt."

I recalled a fundraising event with him last week, but no one at the station had attended the event. "What about him?" I asked.

"It would seem that you have some potential blackmail footage. The man Green interrogated said he was ordered to kill you and take your equipment."

Cyan swallowed and chimed in. "In other words, we're on the right track and, thanks to you, we've actually gotten a head start."

I felt a glow of pride at my deduction. "I'm happy to help!"

After about ten minutes of sifting through the files once again, I decided to take a step back. Assuming, for the time being, that the footage was of the senator himself, where would he have shown up? Not the cupcake story. Not the grass fire. Not at a robbery scene or crash. I reached into my memory and, starting with the most recent, sifted through every story I had covered.

My phone rang, breaking my trance and startling me. I must have been staring at the computer screen without doing anything for some time. I looked at the number as I straightened. The station again. What was it this time?

"Hello again, Noah," I answered.

"Actually, this is Suzanne." Why on earth would my boss be calling me? She was supposed to be on the air in – I glanced at the clock in the corner of the computer screen – twenty-three minutes. "Have you seen Noah?"

"We spoke a few hours ago. He was at the station. Why? Is he not there?"

"No. And he deleted some of our archives before he left. The entirety of last week."

The feeling of icy water being poured slowly down the back of my neck quickly spread to my spine and out. The government. My mind raced with possibilities. What had they done to him? Was he one of them? No, there was no proof. No proof of anything. I couldn't say anything to Suzanne without evidence or at least citing my sources. Any other friend, maybe, but not the News Director.

"Anna?"

I snapped back to the conversation. "Sorry. That's weird. Everything seemed fine when I talked with him." It wasn't exactly a lie, but I still felt bad deceiving her. "I'll let you know if I hear from him, though." I hoped beyond reason that I would, but the sinking feeling in my gut contested that wish.

"Okay, thanks. I'll do the same for you." Suzanne's voice echoed more annoyance at Noah's absence than concern.

"Thanks."

The click at the other end was still audible as I slowly lowered my phone. I noticed Limey eyeing me through the stacks of equipment.

"Everything alright?" he asked.

"One of my coworkers went missing with some of our archives."

"Really?" Cyan piped up, his head appearing from behind a computer screen.

"Which archives?" Really? That was the question he was asking?

"All of last week," I answered, incredulous.

"Cool. That narrows it down." I wanted to slap Limey for his coldness toward the news.

Cyan must have noticed my irritation. "Whether your friend took the archived shows or was a victim of the one who took it, there's nothing we can do. But by taking the footage, they narrow down our search. From three and a half weeks to one." The conclusion made sense, but I still couldn't help but be perturbed.

"What did you cover last week?" Limey asked.

I searched my memory, and found the only thing that made sense. The city council meeting. They were discussing a quarter-cent tax hike. What did that have to do with Senator Lewitt? "Tuesday was the city council meeting," I answered anyway.

Cyan nodded. "We'll start there."

"I'll look at the live shots," I announced. We didn't need to overlap our searches just yet.

"I'll take the council room," Limey stated. That left Cyan with the man-on-the-street reactions. I donned my headphones and got to work.

I watched the live shots, familiar with the story, but nothing stood out. If it wasn't the content of the story proper, it must have been something in the background. I watched it again, but everything in sight was ordinary. Half the background was shrouded by the building's shadow, but it was too dark to discern.

Maybe sound? I played it again, this time closing my eyes and just listening. I felt simultaneous pride and annoyance. There was very little background audio captured by the mic. It was a difficult goal for any live shot, but I had achieved it. Unfortunately that meant there was little information there at all, and nothing useful.

Maybe the darker sections? I opened my eyes and stared. I would need some digital help. I found the brightness and contrast controls on their video playback program and adjusted them. Now the shot of myself at the center of the screen was bright white and way over-exposed, but the darker corners lit up showing a fair amount of detail despite the graininess from the change.

There he was – Senator Lewitt, talking with a woman I didn't recognize. The video had been paused when I adjusted it, but it was clear the pair were not happy with each other.

I found it. Whatever it was they were hiding was here.

"Hey, guys," I said, glancing up and pulling my headphones off. They were both engrossed in their work. "Guys." I stepped toward Cyan to pull off his headphones, too. The movement caught the attention of both them and they stood, shedding the tethers to their computers. "Take a look at this."

I unplugged my headphones so they could hear, even though the audio was useless. I pointed at the corner of the screen that held the Senator.

"Bingo!" Cyan said under his breath.

I hit the spacebar to play the video. The fact that Senator Lewitt was there wasn't suspicious enough to kill over. It had to be something he did while he was there. The screen sprang into action.

The woman was arguing with him, and tensions escalated quickly. She reached up suddenly and slapped him. I jumped in spite of myself, but didn't dare blink.

The Senator absorbed the blow and turned back to her slowly. She was still vehemently making her point. Once he straightened fully again, he rocked his right shoulder back and landed a closed fist on her jaw. The woman's head twisted awkwardly in place for a moment before it bounced back.

Another woman entered the scene, grabbing the senator's young assailant at the base of her ponytail and pulled downward to expose her neck. The senator watched, as did my co-conspirators and I, as the blonde woman pierced a needle into the brunette's neck.

To my surprise, the video froze. I looked down to notice the arrow was at the end of the timeline. Cyan let out a low whistle and Limey a "That'll do it."

We needed to copy it. "Do either of you have a flash drive?" Immediately the scene broke and Cyan was moving back to his end of the desk and opening drawers.

"I agree," he said as he dug. He spotted one, tossed it to me, and continued digging. I didn't feel obligated to point out that there was nothing I said for him to agree to. I knew what he meant.

"I'll go tell Saturday," Limey said as he ducked out.

I saved the new setting so that the copies would have the scene with the Senator clearly visible. It didn't take long before backup copies had been scattered around the office building and stored digitally on the cloud.

Sunday

4

Black slept quickly and without trouble, for once. Maybe it was the lack of sleep from the night previous or the eventful day. Either way, he went to bed the moment he got home, barely taking his shoes off before finding the pillow.

It was the middle of the night when he woke up. The neighborhood was unusually quiet. He closed his eyes and breathed in the calmness, debating if he should try to go back to sleep or turn a fan on to make noise.

Suddenly a sickly sweet smell overwhelmed his senses. He knew that scent: chloroform. Black opened his eyes again and instinctively tried to separate himself from the cloth bearing down on him with the scent. A blonde woman stood above him, face uncovered, putting her weight on to Black to fight his strength.

Black twisted, rolling to his side, and pulled the cloth and woman away, throwing them to the ground. He could already feel the chemical sapping his strength. He needed air. With more effort than he would ever admit, Black stood and faced the woman, now standing over her. He could feel his wits and strength returning. It was too slow.

Quick as a snake, Black felt more arms wrap his elbows from behind him. It took far too long for him to realize that there was a third person in the room. This new attacker brought Black's elbows together, locking his arms behind him and lifting. Black grasped for any sensitive areas or pressure points to employ and free himself, but all he managed to catch was a fistful of shirt with Kevlar underneath.

Still facing the woman and his bed, Black could only watch as the blonde stood again, brushed herself off, and picked up the cloth she had placed over his mouth earlier. She seemed to contemplate it for just a moment, then lunged at him with a quick ferocity. Black held his breath before the cloth landed, but she looked him in the eye, patiently waiting for the chemical to take effect.

Fury boiled up inside Black, but he could do little more than rock his shoulders from this position. Kicking her wouldn't get the goon behind him to let go. More likely he'd tighten his grip and dislocate Black's shoulders.

Finally, Black could not hold his breath any longer, and he saw his attacker smile slightly as he resigned, breathing in the chemical.

Black had no idea how long it was before he awoke again. A bump jolted him awake, and it only took him moments to figure out he was in a car. He had been folded up and tucked in the fetal position in what seemed to be a plastic tub just large enough to hold him. Zip ties held his wrists together in front of him; the same kind Black had stolen from and used against his attacker yesterday. Apparently they were standard issue with this crowd.

Black felt the corners of the tub, searching for an opening. The box must have a lid. Above him. He probably should have guessed that. Slowly and patiently he pressed his way around the seal, searching for weak spots. More than once Black felt the entire tub bounce and slide with the jostle of transport. The lid seemed evenly attached all the way around. That meant tape or glue instead of ropes or a latch. No scent of glue.

The edges of the tub bowed under Black's weight.

He felt the vehicle slow nearly to a stop, then proceed again. Some sort of checkpoint? More likely a stop sign.

One minute and windy road later, the vehicle stopped entirely. Black waited, biding his time, for them to take him out. Five minutes passed uneventfully, then ten. Black knew from personal experience how inefficiently the government could be run, but really? It was already getting warm.

The air grew closer and hotter. No amount of shifting made the plastic coffin any larger or more comfortable. Black could wait – he knew he had no other choice. Whether the warm temperature or the lack of breathable air was the cause, Black couldn't tell, but he could feel himself being dragged toward sleep.

He fought it, but still it beckoned. Black twisted his wrists until the Zip ties pinched his skin in order to keep himself awake and alert. Even that only helped briefly.

Black couldn't tell if it had been an hour or ten by the time he heard the trunk or rear door open and felt the tub being dragged out of the vehicle. They toted the box, with Black inside, around for a few minutes.

When the lid finally opened, Black was dumped into air conditioning and onto unforgiving tile. Immediately trying to get his bearings, he looked up. His vision was filled with the face of the woman he had fought – if you could call it that – earlier.

"Hey there. It's okay," she cooed.

Venom boiled up in Black. He was not some lost dog!

Black spat at her. The majority of it landed on her forehead above her right eye. How dare she put him in this position and act like she was a friend?

She wiped it away. "That's no way to treat a lady." The woman stood up and walked toward the room's only door, leaving him to his own devices. Black seized his chance and clambered the rest of the way out of the tub, wrists still bound. The sudden movement after being still for so long made his muscles clamp up. Any effort to stand was thwarted and Black crumpled to the ground. Not starting from any height, he did not fall hard.

"It's okay. There you go." She patted him on the back like Black was her pet.

Black shied away and cleared his throat, collecting his thoughts and his voice. "Don't you dare touch me." His voice sounded hoarse, even to him. Thirst. He needed water.

The woman, as if reading his thoughts, stood fully and walked to a water bottle she had some distance away. She shook it as she brought it back, opened it as she knelt, and offered it to him.

Black wanted it, he really did. But his better sense took over and he looked away. "Go to hell."

"I confess," she said as she freed his hands from the Zip ties, "I put sodium pentothal in it. I'd hoped that it would smooth this transition back home for you." Truth serum, as it was known. Not a chance.

"Home?" Black spat. "You took me away from my home."

"Where you sleep is not always your home." The woman moved back into view, water bottle still in hand. "Think of me as your mother. I won't hurt you unless you make me." She was maybe a year older than him. The last time Black's mother had been that age was when he – Black did the math – was six years old.

Stop it! Black scolded himself. Focus!

The woman eyed him perceptively. "You don't trust me. I get it. But you should." She loosened the cap and drank deeply from the water bottle. Black could only stare from his half-raised position on the floor. "There. I'll tell the truth. Ask anything you want." The clear plastic was held on display between them, showing the liquid half-drained.

Black knew that it would take five minutes or so for it to get into the bloodstream. Then he could trust her. The woman who called herself his mother held the water bottle to him. At least he knew it wasn't poisoned. If she could stand up to it, so could he. The desire for liquid was too much – Black took the bottle and drained the remnants. It tasted like salty Listerine, but he managed to keep it down.

There were no chairs in the room, so the two of them sat on the floor, staring at each other. A minute passed in utter silence, then more. Black looked around the room. It was an official interrogation chamber, complete with cameras and a one-way mirror. It felt like a cage. Or a kennel.

Then the woman moved a hand toward his head. Black instinctively shied away.

"It's okay," she said, still holding her hand aloft. "Your hair is out of place. I just want to fix it."

Black nodded. He closed his eyes and endured her touch.

"Who's a good boy?" she asked as she combed her fingers through his hair.

"I am," Black answered without thinking. Really?

"Yes, you are."

"The sodium pentothal is working already." Why? Why would he announce that? Black chided himself, but his common sense filter seemed to be gone.

The woman's eyes lit up. "I know it is. I have a secret for you. I'm not your mother."

"I know." Black then realized he could ask her any questions, too. "Who are you?"

"My name is Natasha. I work for Senator Lewitt." Black knew that, didn't he? Not the first, but the second part. "Tell me something about you," she bid.

"My first name is Humphrey," Black said. The words just sort of made their way out of his mouth, unbidden.

"Humphrey?" She laughed and combed her hand through his hair again. The whole scene felt like the first time he had gotten a girl drunk, the night before he went into boot camp.

What? What should he ask her? Their location. That would be useful. "Where are we?"

"We call it the office. It's about ten miles outside of town." She answered instantly and without hesitation. "Where did you take our man?"

"To the office building downtown. The one under construction. Blue has probably relocated him to the jail by now." Black instantly regretted the words, even as he spoke them. He just couldn't stop them. "My turn." What to ask next? "Is Senator Lewitt your boss?"

"Yup."

"Who's his boss?"

"Uh, uh," the woman, Natasha, chided him. "My turn first. Is your boss the one they call Saturday or Tuesday?"

"Saturday. I like to think we all work for the betterment of the public at large, though. That's why I joined the Air Force. I wanted to help people." Black gave up in his fight with himself to withhold information. It wasn't helping in the least anyway. His turn. "Is anybody giving orders to the Senator?"

"Not that I'm aware of. Will you behave for me when I leave the room? I want you to behave."

"No." Black was already contemplating his escape.

The room was well-proofed. The hinges on the door were on the outside. Nothing besides the two of them in the room. And the plastic tub. No chairs to use as a tool. The window didn't even have a lip on it to help Black cut any bonds that would hold his hands together, should she replace them.

"Why are you being honest with me? Are you going to kill me?" And with that, Black's lack-of-filter exposed a fear and a weakness. It was remarkable how rarely he interrogated people of value who cared about their own lives more than the cause. But there it was.

"Yes, I plan to kill you. Does that bother you?"

"Yes. If anyone said no, I'd say they were lying."

"We all care about number one in the end, don't we?" She stopped playing with his hair. "One more question each. Your turn."

One left? Black asked the question in the front of his mind without contemplating its merits fully. "How do I escape?"

"Escape? Easily. Obey me. Call me mother. If so, we'll let you go. All we want from you is your allegiance." She had to be telling the truth, hadn't she? The blonde Natasha that wanted Black to call her "mother" stood and brushed herself off, looking down on him. "My turn. Tell me what you know about the reporter."

Having spent hours researching her yesterday, Black had a lot to tell.

Blackmail.

Just the word made my stomach sink. That was exactly what I had on the senator.

What could I do with it? Pretend like nothing ever happened? That was somehow worse. Like I was helping cover a conspiracy. I needed to report it. But what I had was a video clip. A start. I needed to get the whole story.

I had stayed awake long into the night, staring at the ceiling from the cot in the break room. I didn't dare go back to my apartment. I could never sleep if I didn't feel safe. Even as a child, I kept a safety blanket longer than I'd ever confess out loud. I still slept with stuffed animals when in my own bed. But the safest place I could be was on that cot, in that office building downtown, so I drifted into an easy sleep.

I awoke the next morning, refreshed with new clarity. The brunette woman. She was the key. If I could get her to go on camera and talk, that would be my story. Supported by the footage we had stashed on every hard drive we trusted.

All the information I had was from that video, but I felt equal to the task ahead of me. I was a reporter, after all. Research and revealing the truth behind any situation was what I did.

Sitting up on the cot, I pulled my hair back to a ponytail with an elastic band I kept on my wrist for just that purpose. Brushing my hair seemed absurd and not my problem right now. I stood and flattened my wrinkled shirt before heading out and down the hall.

I nearly didn't look up in time as I walked to the computer room I had worked in yesterday. I stopped short of another man, one that I had met before, but not in this building.

"Officer Ratledge," I said, surprised.

He seemed just as surprised to see me. "Anna? What are you doing here? This building is still under construction."

I gave him what must have been an awkward and blank stare as I struggled to find a lie that explained my presence. I had never lied to an officer of the law before. "I was just looking for a restroom." It was a lame story, and I knew it.

"On the fourth floor?"

"I found one when I came in on the first floor, but I got turned around." Silver would let me back in, wouldn't he? If it got so far as Ratledge booting me out, that is. But at least it would get the officer away from the operation.

It was then that I noticed Cyan turn the corner behind the policeman and approach them. A sigh of relief washed over and escaped me. Cyan could handle it. Ratledge must have seen the change in me, because he turned to seek the cause.

"I'm taking care of this," the officer said without preamble. Despite finding me at the wrong place, he seemed protective over me.

"I'm glad you two have met," Cyan said, approaching the conversation.

"It's okay that she's here?" Ratledge asked.

"She's helping us on a project, Blue." Cyan spoke with authority.

A look of pleasant surprise washed over the officer's face, echoing my own feelings. Ratledge was a part of this! We were all on the same side.

"I thought you were on patrol today," Cyan commented, turning the focus away from me and back to the officer. He was "Blue" here. Made sense, as he was an officer of the law, inevitably dressed in dark blue.

"I am. This was important, though. The man you had me bring in yesterday is out on bail already."

"That was fast," I commented. Out on bail over the weekend, much less a Sunday?

"He must have had help," Cyan proposed.

"I just wish the bad guys would stay in jail," Blue said, frustration clearly evident. "Who all does he know here?"

"Black and Green interrogated him."

"And he saw me," I chimed in.

"You're likely his biggest target," Cyan said. "It'd be smart to stay here."

I shrugged. My next step could be done here, but I didn't plan on staying cooped up if my research led me into the field.

"I already told Green," Blue said. "But I couldn't find Black. Is he here?"

"Let's ask Silver," Cyan said. "I've not seen Black yet today." He spoke as we walked. "Which is odd. Normally he beats me here."

"Maybe he has a life? Not all of us here are trust fund babies." Blue joked, but I could see Cyan bristle.

Looking at Cyan, suddenly his presence here made sense. I could see it in his hair gel and posture. He came from wealth. Maybe it was the taxes or the rules of the federal government that he despised, but this was personal. Then again, I supposed it was personal for all of us in one way or another. Blue had to be irritated with the way the federal government kept stepping on the toes of the local government. I'd heard Black and Green were both ex-military, and had to be fed up with how things were run, even if what they stood for still held true.

"Well, Black is retired. He has nothing in his life that I know of but this organization," Cyan mused. "Maybe I just missed him."

The three of us approached Silver at the elevator. He stood placidly, leaning on a cane. "Black isn't here yet," he said, either anticipating the question or just stating a fact. The first, I decided after looking at him a moment.

"Weird. Okay, I'll call him in a minute," Cyan stated, releasing the officer from his duty to inform Black of the situation.

Blue nodded farewell to me and entered the elevator.

First Noah, then Black? None of it sat well with me. My concern must have been evident because Cyan walked me to our work station from yesterday and spoke. "He's fine. He can handle himself. He likely just slept in."

I detected some concern in his voice, too, and it was clear he cared about his comrade more than he confessed. Finding the same chair I occupied last time, I sat. Limey wasn't anywhere around, and Cyan pulled out his phone and stepped away, leaving me at my station.

The woman. I opened the internet and started my search for her.

5

The next time Black saw "Mother" must have been hours later. No. Natasha. He couldn't start falling into her trap. Black stood up when he saw her enter.

"You have a very persistent friend," she said as she sauntered over. "He's called three times in the last hour."

Friend? Black didn't have friends. The closest he had were associates, and those were at the organization. Mother showed him the phone. Three missed calls and one voicemail, all from Cyan. It was at times like this Black was grateful for the code names. This woman may hear his voice, but would never understand who he was.

She pulled the phone back, entered his passcode into the cell, and looked at it without sharing. How did she get the code to his phone? He assumed it wasn't hard to figure out – his squadron number from when he was in the Air Force. That meant they knew who he was. Mother put the cell on speakerphone and let it play the voicemail.

"Hello Black. This is Cyan. We could use your help on a project. Call me when you get this." It was sufficiently vague. He was clever, for who he was. He must be suspect of Black's absence now.

"What happens next?" Mother asked, pocketing the phone.

"They start looking for me." Black knew they would go to his place first, and of course find it empty. As each member joined the organization, they opted in or out of letting the organization track their locations via their phone. Naturally suspicious of everything, Black had opted out, though he wished now that he hadn't.

"How soon?"

Black had no idea, to be honest. But fortunately the truth serum had run its course and he was able to think before answering again. "Immediately."

Black watched the woman study him, guessing if he was telling the truth or not. "Call him," she demanded, pulling the phone out again and handing it to him.

Black took and held it for a moment. "And tell him what?" Black had full memory of the conversation earlier and could easily relay the information he had acquired to the organization. If he was forthright about it, though, the government would know. They'd slaughter them, and easily. Black couldn't put his friends in that kind of danger. Not again. Hopefully Cyan remembered some of the codes they had established.

"That you're okay and to call off the search," Mother answered.

Black accepted the phone and called Cyan back.

"There you are! What are you doing?" Cyan answered the phone without salutation.

"I'm fine. I decided to get out of town and get some fresh air. I'm hiking today." Black maintained eye contact with the woman opposite him as he spoke. She gave no indication that she disapproved of what he had said. Black hoped, however, that Cyan had caught on. First, that something was wrong. Black hated the mountains and much preferred the bustle of the city. The rural area was far too quiet, he had once confessed to Cyan. The second was the outside of town hint. Black wasn't so sure he would get that one.

"Oh, okay." Cyan sounded casual. Too casual, if you knew him. Fortunately Cyan was a skilled actor. "Did you want me to pick up lunch for you?" Good. He had picked up on Black's distress call, at least. The line was code, asking him in no uncertain terms that he was being held captive. A "no" answer meant yes, and vice versa, and any time included in the response was to tell them how many captors he had seen.

"No, I'm going to be away until at least one. Maybe out as far as ten." Black hoped Cyan would make the connection with the "out of town" and "as far as ten" to give the organization a search radius.

Mother leveled a gaze at him, warning him not to be too open.

"Look, I've got to go," Black said. Anything more that he would try to communicate would only rouse suspicion.

"Okay," Cyan responded. "I'll see you tomorrow then." That wasn't code for anything, but in light of their other communication, Black hoped it meant they understood and would be coming for him. He would just have to hold out.

"Or the next day," Black said. He could last here for two days if it meant the rest of the organization stayed safe.

"Okay." There was a click on the phone as Cyan hung up on the other side.

Black brought the phone down from his ear and hung up, too. Mother snatched it from him and pocketed it before he could do anything else. She turned to leave and immediately spun back, giving him a large, false smile.

"Good boy," she said, patting him twice on the head. Her touch gave him mixed feelings, and Black didn't know quite what to make of it. Yes, hers was the only touch of a human he had felt – besides a fight – in ages, and yes, part of him longed for approval as any human would. But a sour flavor struck him as he recognized who it was that he sought approval from. Black turned his head away in disgust, more at himself than at the woman who had patted him.

Mother left, leaving Black utterly by himself again. A bitter loneliness fell over him. Two days. It felt like a lifetime. No. He would wait it out. He would beat them at their own game. There was no way Mother would win.

Black refused to let the silence overwhelm him, and instead started doing push-ups, letting his own breathing be his symphony.

A horrible thought struck me as I researched, looking for the unknown woman. If they were willing to kill me for merely filming the exchange, what were the chances this brunette still lived? Cyan left me alone with the internet for a couple hours after receiving a phone call and I hadn't seen him since.

I assessed what I knew about the woman thus far. She was younger than me, maybe 21 or 22. She wasn't part of Lewitt's staff – I had checked through the pages on his campaign website and couldn't find her. The woman who had drugged her had to be under his service in some way, but wasn't listed either. Senator Lewitt's head of security was listed as a someone else entirely.

We already had a name and mug shot of one of the crew, but that wasn't really of any use to us. Maybe Green could help? He apparently knew the enemy and their operations better than anyone, and my research had plenty of rabbit holes I could follow, but none proved a promising lead.

I stood and stretched, looking toward the door. Cyan had not returned yet, but I didn't need an escort.

I found Silver in his usual spot, staring at nothing in particular. At first I thought he was listening to music, because he definitely didn't seem present mentally. Except there were no ear buds dangling from his ears and certainly no music audible.

"Silver? Am I interrupting something?" I asked, trying to be as gentle and demure as possible. Startling the wrong person here could be a dangerous move.

"Hello, Anna," he said, turning slightly and snapping out of his trance without jumping. "Not interrupting anything important. I was merely playing chess. What can I do for you?"

"Do you know where I might find Green?"

"He and Saturday are in the room down the hall." His phone beeped, and he paused to pull it out and glance at it. "Well, how about that. Saturday wants to see you."

"Me?" I asked, alarmed. What had I done?

"Yes, miss. Don't worry. Down the hall, on the right."

I pointed to where I thought he meant, and he nodded. Okay then. I straightened my shirt and pulled out my hair, attempting to appear presentable. Then, remembering I hadn't brushed through it since I had woken up, pulled it back again.

I hesitated at the door. Should I knock or just go in? I had been summoned after all. People here, in my recollection at least, never knocked. They just sort of came and went as they pleased.

I wasn't them, though, so I knocked. I waited for a second as steps approached the door and instinctively tugged at my t-shirt again. Green opened the door with a look of pleasant astonishment on his face before beckoning me in.

"Sorry." I wasn't even sure what I was apologizing for, except that he was surprised at my appearance.

"Not at all. Silver is quick, but I didn't expect him to send you that quickly." I didn't want to spoil the praise for Silver by explaining what had happened. I was saved any opportunity by Green, who called my attention to the third person in the room. "This is Saturday. And this is Anna Pitt."

For all the power this man held, Saturday looked remarkably normal. A little older than Black or Cyan, but not yet nearing Silver's age. Premature balding, maybe a little overweight. Cleanly but simply dressed.

The man smiled and stood, offering his hand for me to shake.

I took it and smiled. This was just like any other interview I had done. Or at least that was what I told myself.

"Nice to meet you," Saturday said as he sat again and scooted his chair in.

"Likewise." I sat on Green's side of the table. Green closed the door again and sat, leaning back in his chair on the other side of me. I felt like I should have questions prepared, but this was no normal interview. I was on the other side of the conversation this time.

"Why're you here, Anna?" Saturday spoke casually, as if they were meeting up for coffee instead of gathering with code names in an otherwise empty building.

What did he mean? Surely he had been informed on the circumstances that had brought me there. I had spent the night here because I didn't want to go home. I pointed my thoughts in another direction before I could dwell on Lucy. I still couldn't bear to think of her.

"I want justice," I spoke, summoning up my entire reason for being there. For being at all. "Not just because they attacked me." Not just because of what they did to my dog. "Not just because that woman that hit Senator Lewitt needs to be found and protected. But because Lewitt needs to face justice. And if I can help with that, I will." I spoke honestly and from the heart. If I said something he didn't like, that was his problem. But I didn't get the impression Saturday nor Green disapproved.

"What has he ever done to you? Did you hate him last week?"

"Before Friday night, he was nothing more than a campaign story to me."

"Anyone else you'd like to face justice?"

What an absurd question. "Why are you asking me this?"

"Answer the question, please," Saturday insisted.

Might as well say it. "The man that killed my dog yesterday. The one that's out on bail today. That's not justice." Miffed, I lost all desire to be presentable to these people. Did they think I was some conspiracy nut? Or maybe someone who wanted to strike down the entirety of anyone who ever rubbed me the wrong way?

"Good." Saturday leaned forward and smiled, putting me at ease again. Okay, I was probably overreacting.

More than that - I had been rude. "Sorry." These men here were not the enemy, and I knew that.

Saturday waved a hand, dismissing my misstep. "While you're here with us, we'd like to address you under another name. We have to be careful, you understand."

I did. "You want to give me a code name. Like a color?" This was for everybody's protection, not just my own. I put a massive target on the organization when I spent time with them, and I knew it.

"Yes. Green here has suggested we call you White. What do you think?"

White. It was the color of purity. And that of transparency. I liked it. It suited me. The truth was what mattered, and I just wanted to be on the side of truth.

I nodded. "This is just temporary, though," I said, wanting to be perfectly clear with them. "Once this whole thing is over, I'm walking away."

"You have that right, of course." Saturday rose as he spoke, and I followed suit. "Though you're very good at what you do, and we hope that you'll elect to stay with us."

"Thank you." I bowed my head in accepting the compliment as he left. Green made to follow him. I touched the muscular man as he passed me, causing him to turn. "Do you have a minute?" I asked once I had his attention.

"Sure." Green turned and waited for me.

"You've seen the video?" I didn't feel like I needed to specify. I wasn't talking about some YouTube cat video, and we both knew it.

"Of course."

"I'm looking to find the woman. If I can get her to go on camera –"

"She's dead. More than likely."

"They killed her?" I asked, appalled.

"You can't seriously think they'd let her live." Green eyed me, likely evaluating my naiveté. I didn't much care about that at the moment, though.

"I'd just hoped…" I didn't know how to conclude.

"The man who tried to kill you yesterday got out on bail today."

"I know."

"He's not exactly going to spend his free time binge-watching Netflix." Green's words were kind to me, but there was an incredulity behind them. "This is a clean-up operation."

"Do you know who she is?" I asked.

"She worked for the catering company for his last fundraising event. I don't know what the argument was about, though."

Finally, a credible lead! I did my best not to be too outwardly excited. "What was her name?" Maybe I could talk to her family and get the whole story.

Green's face was one of concern, and perhaps a little bit of pity. "Liza Strating. Why?"

"I have a very different way of bringing down someone than you do. You can kill him, but I can expose him. Together, I think we can stop him."

Green grinned at my little speech. "Sounds good. Keep me up to date, White."

I smiled, pleased to be addressed by my code name. It definitely suited me.

6

A gentle buzzing started not long after Mother left with Black's cell phone. At first, it sounded distant. Black spent a considerable amount of time trying to narrow down its source, but to no avail. It seemed to be everywhere and nowhere. For a while Black contemplated that he himself might be the source, but if so, it would have to be his own brain generating the sound in order to keep the world from being too quiet.

He eventually gave up and sat, resigned to the sound and his circumstances. Every idea for escape that crossed his mind was quickly followed with a reason why it wouldn't work. Mother had freed his hands, so he should be able to. He just had to figure out how.

Breaking the glass in the only window in the room would be impossible. Even if he somehow managed it, it would lead to yet another locked door and just a slightly larger cage. Ceiling tiles were always a good place to start, but the ones that capped this room were too far away, even if he jumped. Black could tell that just by looking.

A water bowl and as-of-yet empty food bowl, both designed for dogs, were the only tools he had available to him. He had his clothes still as well, if it became necessary to use those, but at the moment Black couldn't see how.

The incessant buzzing was just loud enough to stick to the forefront of his attention. It distracted Black from any long veins of thought as he waited. But, then again, it wasn't like Black was in any hurry.

He found himself looking forward to Mother's next visit. There was something intoxicating about her presence.

Scarlett could learn something from her. Mother was obviously an accomplished chemist to some extent. The sedation serum on the reporter, chloroform on him, then the sodium pentothal. What else did she have in store? Was she already working some sort of scheme?

Then it hit him. Her perfume. It didn't take much for Black to conjure the memory, though he had never particularly focused on it before. It was simply another detail, like the gentle curl in the golden hair. The perfume had a sweet, floral scent. Maybe it was something about that chemical compound that made him crave her. Or simply his need to interact with people, and she was his lifeline to the rest of the world. Black would have to wait until she returned to analyze it.

Until then, he sat in the corner of the room, thinking, able to watch both the window – where he assumed others watched him back – and the door, where any physical threat would have to approach him.

Thirst gnawed at him, and Black's gaze shifted frequently to the dog bowl filled with water. But, after yesterday's interrogation of the government's man, Black more than knew better.

So, Black waited, thirsty, contemplating Mother and her presence.

Scarlett sat next to Cyan, watching the map projected on the wall as he explained the odd phone call with Black. They had two days before Black would be expecting them. That much was clear. He had also told Cyan with the established code that he had only seen one interrogator, but there were inevitably more people at the facility that held him. The information wasn't actually good news, either. It meant, when the time came, they couldn't fake access without looking exactly like his captor.

Scarlett realized she had been chewing on a rather large dry erase marker as she thought, so she pulled it out and leaned forward. The room had been quiet for a couple minutes as she and Cyan contemplated the problem.

"Ten," Cyan said, suddenly standing up. "Maybe the hiking statement has nothing to do with it. Maybe the ten he dropped does." Scarlett watched as Cyan scooted his chair back and stood, head blocking the path of the projector slightly.

"Are you thinking an address?" she asked. "I doubt there are any two-digit addresses in the city." The marker ended up back in her mouth, and she chewed it thoughtfully.

"More likely a radius. If he actually is out of town, then maybe ten is a distance?"

"Miles or minutes?"

"It depends on how he got the information."

Then a thought struck her. It didn't matter. "The speed limit outside of town is...?"

"Fifty-five," Cyan answered immediately. He was a car guy, like she was, and as a native to this town, he probably had every speed limit in the area memorized. "Which means they were probably going sixty." A mile a minute.

They were thinking in tandem now. Scarlett stood, pointing with the shadow of her finger at the projected map. "That means somewhere along this line."

Cyan grabbed a dry erase marker and circled any roads that intersected with the radius she had drawn with her shadow. Seven. Three to the east, all near each other. Two freeways to the south and southwest with several buildings as options in that area. The highway that led west and the one that led north each had no significant crossroads.

"We need Green to narrow this down." Scarlett leaned forward, hands on the desk in front of them, and twisted, stretching. It pleased her to notice she had distracted Cyan with the movement.

Cyan blinked and reached for the phone, putting it on speaker and calling Green. It rang once before the Army Ranger picked up.

"Hi," Cyan said, leaning in to make sure he was heard. "Do you have a moment?"

"Sure. Is Black alright? He's officially been targeted, according to my sources."

"That's the trouble," Cyan said. Scarlett coughed, reminding Cyan to tell Green she was in the room too. "You're on with Scarlett, also, by the way. We've narrowed down where they're holding Black to seven locations." Cyan listed off the potential addresses.

"I'll look into it," Green said from the speaker. "I've a target to chat up here, first."

"Can I help?" Scarlett asked, admittedly eager to be doing anything useful. Her talents were wasted cooped up in this office building.

"Come on down. The usual place."

"I'll be there in fifteen." Scarlett left Cyan to clean up the room, pausing only momentarily to wait for the elevator and let Silver know her plans.

In no time at all she pulled up to the local billiards parlor, a frequent hangout for many, including the government agents. Scarlett loved the Porsche Carrera Cabriolet she pulled up in. It was dark red, like her code name, and went from zero to sixty in 4.8 seconds. It may belong to Cyan, but he never insisted that she give back the keys, so she didn't. That, and it drew attention wherever she went, which she relished.

It beeped as she walked away from the parking lot and into the pool hall, turning heads the whole way. Green sat at the bar in the forward part of the room, napkin to his right. That's where he wanted her to sit. Scarlett pulled out her compact and touched up her lipstick as she walked, using the mirror to scope the room. She had everyone's attention, even

Green. Taking her time, Scarlett trotted over and dropped her purse exasperatedly on the bar.

"I am so over him!" She took what was left of Green's drink and drained it. Tonic water. Yuck. "I'll tell you this," she said handing the empty glass back to him, "his mother should have thrown him out and kept the stork," she quoted.

"Marilyn Monroe?" Green asked.

"Nice try. Mae West."

"Can I buy you a shot?" the man behind her asked. Green gave the slightest of nods, indicating to her that he was her target.

"Anything but Jack," she said, spinning to face him. "Jack needs to die."

The bartender brought a shot over. Scarlett snatched it and threw it back without looking at it. Tequila with a twist of lime. Scarlett exhaled, letting the alcohol refresh her, and leaned forward, aware that she was giving him a clear view of her intentionally chosen low-cut shirt.

"My name is –" he started.

"I don't care. Let's play." She reached past him with one arm, lightly brushing her victim, and snatched a pool cue off the wall. Laying her trap, she ran her finger down the side of the cue. The man snapped out of his stupor and stood, flattening his pants unnecessarily.

"Anything the lady wants," the man said to the bartender as he headed to a table to play.

Scarlett smiled and winked at Green as she followed her prey.

Liza Strating. I wasn't able to confirm her death with my research, but it was possible her body hadn't been found yet, much less reported.

I couldn't help but hope she might still be alive. After all, he was only released in the morning, and I was pretty good at what I did. If there was a tiny chance, however slim, that I could beat him to her, I had to try.

Her Facebook profile just listed the town I was currently in as her hometown, but no address. A workplace that I already knew. Her family, who also lived in town.

All the government had to do was find an address on her driver's license. Even if that was just a P.O. Box, the Post Office required a physical address and was also owned by the government. One phone call, maybe two, and they were on their way.

I was about to close out the Facebook tab and see if I could approach the situation from the work front when I glanced at the posts on Liza's wall. Three of the last four posts were tags in pictures, all from her sister. They spanned across several events: one at Starbucks, another at some sort of house party. Perhaps this sister was the key. The government could look up Liza's address, but they wouldn't necessarily care about her as a person. If I had a friendship like this to lean on, I would likely have gotten Lucy and gone to their place to hide instead.

Lucy. The familiar sadness swelled in my throat. No. I couldn't cry. Not again, not now. I had things to do. I took a deep breath, focusing myself, and clicked on the name of the sister.

Manni Thomas. Married with one kid and two cats. Manni appeared to be a stay-at-home mom who threw house parties every chance she could. She and Liza had started a graphic design business that they still ran on the side when Liza wasn't working full time at the only real catering business in town.

Together, Manni and Liza were obviously sisters and best friends. It was definitely the place I'd hide out if I were in a similar pinch. Regardless, if someone knew what had happened to Liza or at least where to start, it'd probably be Manni.

It took me another twenty minutes to search through all the photos taken to find what I was looking for: a home address in a party last spring and the crossroads in a picture that showed off Halloween decorations in the front lawn. Now I had a location.

She lived relatively nearby – about sixteen minutes' travel time, if the map app on my phone was any indicator. I gathered my things to head out but got stopped at the elevator by a cane held horizontally across my path.

"What is this?" I asked Silver, surprised at his audacity to impede me.

"Orders are orders. You aren't supposed to go out unprotected. Sorry, miss." He wasn't really sorry at all. I knew that they had said that, but I thought they just wanted me to be cautious.

"I'll be careful," I said. Silver's cane stayed extended, blocking my way. "Please. A woman's life is in danger. I think I may know where to find her before they reach her. Let me do for her what you've done for me."

My words seemed to have impacted him, and I wondered at his story momentarily. Had he been protected, saved by this organization like I had? Silver hesitated before answering, though. "Maybe we can find someone to go with you."

I nodded, allowing Silver to lower his cane and pull out his phone. He gave a brief explanation to who I presumed was Saturday, paused, said "Yes, sir," and hung up. "He's calling Blue to join you."

Officer Ratledge. He might prove useful. I contented myself to sit on the folding chair across from Silver until the elevator doors opened with the policeman inside. Blue beckoned me and I joined him, ready to help and have help.

Black sat, hunched in the corner of the interrogation room barely able to think over the buzzing. It seemed to swell, loud enough to make sleep impossible. Simple thoughts took enormous effort to follow. He had trained himself to focus on, not filter out his environment.

On top of that, the temperature seemed to be dropping, but only a little. Maybe it was just that Black had moved only minimally in the last few hours. Or they were just starting to strain his body. They had already begun to with this mind. He felt it happen but knew he was helpless to fight it.

Suddenly, after far too long of staring at nothing, the door opened and two things happened. First, and most noticeably, Mother walked into the room and directly to his corner. Secondly, Black noticed the buzzing sound dropped almost entirely. It was still there, in the background, but it felt like the anchor that held his thoughts captive underwater had just let him go. They rushed to the surface, gulping for sanity. When the woman approached, she touched him on the head, flattening his hair again before kneeling in his line of sight.

"Hello Black," Mother said, stroking his arm. There was something familiar about her touch. No. Black shook himself physically. He couldn't have those thoughts.

Mother recoiled at his movement, but did not shy away from Black entirely. "What do you want this time?" Black wondered aloud. She was still the enemy, and being abrasive was about his only tool against this woman. He just had to hold on. Don't fall, don't tell them anything more. He needed to outlast her, but if he was honest with himself, he was losing that battle.

"I want you to be happy. I'm your mother, remember?" She wasn't, and he knew that, but that wasn't a battle Black cared about winning at the moment. She stood slowly, watching him as he watched her. "I've a gift for you. Would you like that? A special treat?" She emphasized the last word slightly. Just a little bit, but Black noticed.

What could she have that he would want? His freedom, of course, but he knew that wasn't going to happen. The chance to use a restroom privately would be nice, so he could finally quench his palate. The odds were not in his favor there, either.

"What is it?" Black's voice sounded hoarse, even to himself. He blamed his current predicament for it. That, and the fact that he hadn't spoken for hours.

"A surprise. But first, you have to do something for me." Black eyed her for a moment, looking up at her as she looked down on him. A thought flashed through his mind then: she could easily knee him in the face from this position. One small move, and at least Black's misery would be suspended, if not over entirely.

The thought left as quickly as it came.

"Stand up." It was half a request, half an order. "That's all I want. You just have to stand up until you're done with your treat. Come on," she coaxed, calling him with her fingers but not offering a hand to help him up. "You can do it. Come on."

Black pondered the situation a moment, then nodded, complying. Why not? Whether from the fight he had been in recently or sitting immobile for hours afterward, Black had far too much trouble standing. He had to brace himself on the wall behind him, taking five full seconds to get upright. Once standing, though, he felt better.

"Good boy," Mother said, smiling broadly at him. "Stay. I'll be right back." She walked to the door and glanced back at him only to command another "stay" before heading out.

Black stood there, staring after the door for a moment. The instant the door closed, the buzzing returned. A part of Black hoped she'd come back quickly, just to take the edge off the incessant sound again.

Black shook his head. No. That was exactly what she wanted.

The movement felt good on his muscles, though. Slowly, meticulously, Black stretched as many of his muscles as he could, one by one. First the shoulders, then the arm. Then the core. That hurt the most, but it was a pleasant kind of pain, releasing his body from its trappings.

He was just beginning to work his way downward, to his legs, when the door opened once more. The last person he expected then came stumbling in. The man he had interrogated last week. No, it was yesterday. Had he really only been in this room since this morning? It felt like ages.

Black watched as the man gained his balance before he fell completely, then stood erect as if nothing had happened. His eyes were red. Was he on some sort of drug? If so, it wasn't likely of his own accord. Mother, with her never-ending cocktail of chemicals, was more likely the culprit. This was his treat? Comradery with a fellow victim of her twisted mind? Black had to confess, he did not understand her play.

"Bowlshia shankey," the man said, glaring at Black.

"What?" he responded, completely confused. It sounded like the man was saying something, but it wasn't in a language Black was familiar with, and he knew his fair share.

The man across from him repeated the gibberish, this time with obvious anger in his voice.

"What do you want?" The man had to understand English – he had spoken it yesterday when Black's role was reversed.

Black was saved trying to interpret any response. Sneering, the agent lunged for Black's throat, arms outstretched and hands ready to claw and tear at his windpipe. The ten feet between them gave Black more than enough time to put his hands up to protect himself, instead blocking and catching one arm in each of his.

Black spun inward, his back toward the man, forcing both of his opponent's arms over Black's shoulder while crossing them. Now the man's elbows were touching each other and locked out. The choice before Black's opponent was between breaking the arm or flipping over Black entirely and into the wall. Black helped him choose, dropping his own weight and popping his hip back into the other man.

Up and over he went, legs bouncing off the wall before landing between where Black stood and where he had spent the last few hours. The thump as the agent landed echoed through the empty room. For a moment, Black considered stomping the skull of the man before him, offered to him as if Black were the altar of some ancient deity.

Instead, he stepped away. He had clearly and easily enough beaten this man twice now. Hopefully he would learn. Black knew better than to turn his back on the man. Instead, he backed into the center of the room, hands up, watching as the agent regained his focus and flipped himself over, staring at Black from all fours like a grizzly bear. Then the agent popped up and became a man again, though no less dangerous in appearance.

He stalked toward Black. Black still desperately hoped he was trying to concede, even if unable to speak. Finally, when he was about to reach him, the agent swept a backhand toward Black's face. Black dodged right, straight into his opponent's left hand. It landed flat, boxing Black's ear and disorienting him. The next instant, while Black was still reflexively pulling his hands up to protect himself, the slap to his ear became a grab, untrimmed nails biting into the flesh behind his ear. The agent torqued Black's head sideways, pulling until the man's thumb was able to jut into Black's eye.

The man's other hand reached for Black's throat again. Pain burned across Black's face, but all he could do was step away. The agent kept right with him, using the steps to press forward and making Black backpedal.

One step, two, then four, Black tried to get his feet back under himself, but the agent pushed too forcefully and still had half of Black's face in the palm of his hand. On the fifth step back, Black hit the wall and the glass from the two-way mirror. The agent had momentum on his side and ended up sandwiching Black between himself and the wall.

Black caught his breath. This man was really going to kill him. There was no way this could end with both of them alive. A part of Black snapped into auto-pilot at that moment. He refused to be the dead one. Black watched, as if in slow motion, through his un-pierced eye, as the agent rocked his right shoulder back, then forward with a punch to Black's throat. In that split second, Black knew he wouldn't be able to dodge or block the strike, but perhaps only divert it.

Time sped up to normal again as Black's forearm made contact with the man's wrist just before the strike landed, pushing it into Black's collar bone instead. Pain exploded through Black's body, followed by a tingling piercing down his arm. His collar bone was most likely fractured, not snapped clean through, but at least he was still alive. For now.

The pain disappeared, either from adrenaline or shock, Black couldn't tell, but he pushed back. He would not be defeated. Not here, not now, not by this man or that woman's devices. Black roared, turning all his energy to ferocity, and swung his arm, elbowing down into the man's heart and forcing him to finally let go of Black's face.

No time to stop. At a glance, Black assessed the situation. The door knob. It was resting horizontally. That was wide enough to do what Black needed.

Black struck the man's chin with an open left palm, barely feeling that he had made contact through the tingling in that arm. A split second later, Black grabbed the man's right shoulder with his right hand, arm horizontal across his opponent's chest, and stepped forward.

Head still snapped back, the agent had no choice but to go exactly where Black chose. They were nearly at a run by the time Black forced the man into the door, and the man's lower spine directly into the door handle. Paralysis struck the man instantly from that point down, collapsing him in a heap at the base of the door. He would be a paraplegic for the rest of his life, which Black would make sure was brief. He laced his fingers through the man's hair with his left, not letting him fall all the way down, and grabbed the unmoving door handle with his right.

Black stepped back, giving himself room to fully bring his knee up into the man's nose. If the man had survived that, Black had to make sure he wouldn't survive the next.

Again and again, Black kneed the man, feeling the bones fracture as each strike landed someplace different. Blood was soaking through the man's shirt and smeared across his face, but Black didn't care. Crunch crunch, like cereal.

He didn't know how many times he had struck the man this way before he snapped out of it. Surprised at himself, he dropped the man's scalp and the door handle.

What had he done?

7

I had found myself on a ride-along with several officers over my career. I had even ridden along with Officer Ratledge once. This was somehow different. I learned during the trip he had been working with the organization at that time. I never would have singled him out as different from the other officers I had worked with. They were all intelligent people dedicated to keeping people safe.

"I wonder how we should approach this," I said aloud as we pulled off the freeway in the white and blue vehicle. Funny, together with the officer, we were "White" and "Blue", too. "I might have better success alone."

"That's probably true," he said as he turned the steering wheel. I had brought my camera with me, and held it close as we leaned gently with the vehicle. It was my weapon, as the handcuffs and gun were for my current companion. "The problem is, I can't protect you from out here. We might be better off if I played the cop and you the reporter."

"It depends," I responded, musing. "She could react one of two ways. She could immediately shut us out, or she could want to tell us everything." I hoped the latter, but that seemed less plausible. It wasn't like the senator had ingratiated public servants to the people I was trying to talk to.

"I could arrest Liza," Blue said, constantly checking his equipment as he drove. Arrest her? They needed to protect, not terrify her. "Assuming she's alive."

"For now, we'll act like she is." I had no evidence either way, but I would insist on that point. "How would arresting her help? And can you do that?"

"I'd have to come up with some reason to arrest her. A viable link to a crime. But from what you've said, she's an upstanding citizen. Once she's arrested, though, she'll be protected. Even if the senator's men would be able to get through, they wouldn't dare hurt her while she's under camera surveillance."

"There was recently a theft at the catering business she works at," I supplied, remembering a story we had reported earlier, maybe last Thursday. "We could do the good-cop-bad-cop routine, and it would give Manni a reason to open up to me." I saw Blue smile. "What?"

"Nothing. You just make it sound like a TV show. It's a good plan." We were pulling up to the suburb, and I instinctively started looking at address numbers. The corresponding house was on the corner, with an open garage and an SUV along the curb.

"Thank you." We parked alongside the house instead of in front of it, in front of the SUV. I started to get out but stopped when I realized Blue wasn't moving. "What is it?"

"There are three cars, and only supposed to be two drivers at the house." He was right. The garage was open, revealing the rear bumpers of two cars within. The third was parked right behind the police cruiser.

"They could own three cars." The one behind us was an SUV, and could be a spare vehicle for outdoor activities.

"People park spare cars in the garage and more frequently used cars behind them. Not beside the house. That's a visitor." Good thing he came along. I wouldn't have thought twice about an extra vehicle. He punched the plate number into one of his numerous pieces of equipment and watched the screen as it processed his request. "Bingo. That car is Liza's. She's here, or at least was at one point. Good instincts."

"Thanks." I was right! All I had done so far was extrapolate from the information I had, but this was the first real evidence to confirm my theories.

I got out and filmed a quick shot of Blue walking up to the front of the yard, knowing it would make for good video once I broke the story. Blue waved me over and I sprinted to catch up. I wanted to film them answering the door, but wouldn't unless I had permission. Surprising someone with a camera was against my personal rules, and only used as a last resort.

"Police," Blue announced himself, knocking on the front door. I heard a dog barking from somewhere within.

"Hush, Duke," came the voice on the other side, presumably to the dog. Someone was definitely home.

Blue knocked again, and the barking renewed.

A moment later the door opened. A man appeared at the door, one hand on the collar of the barker. "Can I help you officer?"

"I'm looking for Manni Thomas and Elizabeth Strating. They're wanted for questioning."

"And who is she?" the husband asked. What was his name again?

"I'm Anna Pitt," I said, switching the camera's weight to my left hand so I could pull out a business card. The man took it and read it. "I'm with the Channel 20 News. I wanted to get Liza's side of the story." I offered my hand, more out of habit than politeness, but the man didn't take it.

"Manni?" he called, pocketing the card.

"May we come in?" Blue asked.

"Of course." He let go of the dog and opened the door for us to come in. Instead of mauling us, as the dog had first threatened, it sniffed us as we passed inside. I didn't recall a dog in the family from their Facebook profile, but Duke seemed trained well enough. Perhaps they were watching him for someone else.

I immediately recognized Manni as she rounded the corner and approached us. She was in a tank top and sweatpants, rolled at her hips.

"What are you doing here?"

"I have some questions about your sister," Blue answered. "Is she around?"

At the mention of Liza, I saw Manni's eyes dart back to where she had come from.

"Come in." Manni guided us away from where she had appeared and into the living room area. "Can I get you a glass of water or something?" I had to smile. Stand-offish as she was, she was still the homemaker.

"No, thank you." Blue was predictably polite and professional. Manni offered us the couch and she and her husband sat in the love seat across from us.

"May I film?" I asked, holding up the camera still strapped to me. The dog sniffed at Blue, but he seemed used to or unaware of the animal's behaviors.

"I'd rather not," the husband said, hand on his wife's for support. "What is this about? We've done nothing wrong."

"Elizabeth is wanted for questioning in regards to a theft that happened last week at her work." Blue sat erect and professional, but I couldn't help but sink into the couches. I slid the camera off my shoulder and kept it in my lap, as I had in the car.

"I think she's innocent," I said, attempting to put our interviewees at ease. Blue shot a glance at me. This was the plan, wasn't it? Good cop, bad cop? Then I noticed the tiniest hint of a smile before he faced the couple again. The look was for their benefit. "I just want to get both sides of the story," I said, sending my own look back at Blue.

"This is about the theft?" Manni let a little relief show through her question. She definitely knew about the senator ordeal. "She told me she was off that day, but suspected Dave." Manni was addressing me. I was already being seen as an ally.

"Do you have a last name for Dave?" Blue asked.

"Stevenson. Steffenson. Something like that."

"Was Liza with you that day?" I asked.

"Yes. We were working on our business."

"Can you corroborate this?" Blue asked the husband, taking notes.

"I was at work." The man eyed what Blue wrote, but said nothing more.

"She and I went to Radio Shack that day. I think she paid by credit card," Manni supplied, still addressing me.

"That's helpful," I said.

"Evidence shows the theft required at least two people."

"Are you implying she's a suspect?" I asked Blue, stirring the pot and showing them that the officer and I weren't exactly seeing eye to eye.

"Why don't you go wait in the car?" Blue told rather than asked me. What was he thinking? Did he suspect I was sincere? Besides, he had locked the car before we came in. I couldn't get back into it if I wanted to.

"I'll walk you out," Manni said, standing. I also stood, glancing back at Blue, confused. He nodded. What was his plan?

I followed Manni, still toting my more-or-less unused camera. To my surprise, Manni stopped and faced me when we were out of earshot of the men.

"Liza's here," she said, glancing behind me to make sure she wasn't noticed.

"Really?" I asked, surprised more at the fact that she was telling me than the revelation of Liza's presence.

"Please, get the truth out there before anyone else gets hurt."

Alarm rocked through me. Anyone else? Who else could they be talking about? How deep did this really spread?

I nodded, swallowing. "That's why I'm here." I followed Manni past the front door to a guest bedroom.

"Liza?" Manni asked gently, opening the door slightly and poking her head in.

"Are they gone?" a frail voice asked from within.

"Not exactly. A reporter's here. She wants to hear what happened." Manni pushed the door open a little wider and invited me in with a gesture of her hand. She then followed me in, making an effort to close the door quietly behind us.

The sight before me struck a chord inside. Liza lay on the bed, but not covered in blankets. She was pale and sickly. Fragile even. Her left cheek boasted a green and yellow bruise. She was not the vibrant person I had seen in the video nor her pictures online.

"Oh, Liza. What did he do to you?" I asked before I could stop myself.

"What do you mean 'he'?" Manni asked, still understandably defensive over her sister.

I collected myself again. I could be honest, right? "Senator Lewitt."

"How do you know about him?" Liza asked, sitting up as best she could in her bed.

"He targeted me, too." I then stood there, confessing all that I knew about what had happened, including the contents of the video, but very careful to leave the organization out of it. We were sisters of sorts, Liza and I, in the same predicament. Not as she and Manni were, but it was very easy to talk to someone who had also suffered at the hands of the senator and his minions.

Manni took more coaxing than Liza did to let me film her. After I agreed to hide her identity until the whole thing was over, she finally agreed. Liza just wanted to see this through, same as I did. I propped the camera on a bureau across from the bed, which was backlit by a bay window and would silhouette her. I hit the red circle, recording everything Liza had to say.

"He came on to me at the fundraiser," Liza explained. "I think he thought I should be flattered, but he was just another creepy old man. I tried being polite, but he didn't take the hint. He..." Liza's voice broke for a moment, but she found her strength again without needing me to prompt her. "He cornered me, but Brian came to my rescue before the senator could do anything. He chased him out. I thought that was the end of it, but Brian never showed back up to work."

I let out a low whistle. The body count for this ordeal kept piling up.

"There was a pretty blonde woman with the senator. I don't know why he chose me instead." That may have been the same woman that had sedated me the other day and Liza the day of the incident I had on tape. "I hunted him down and found him at the city hall. When I asked him about it, he acted as if he had never seen me." A sigh escaped the broken woman, and her gaze drifted down to her hands. "I just wanted to know what happened to Brian. He refused to answer. Then I hit him. I don't know what came over me. I was just so angry at the whole situation, especially at Senator Lewitt. Then, he hit me back." She pointed out the bruise that colored nearly a quarter of her face. "I... I don't really know what happened next."

"That blonde woman drugged you," I supplied. I had seen it in the video. "She drugged me too, but later." I pulled my collar down to show the tiny bruise where the needle had punctured my neck.

I could see the rage combat weakness in the woman in front of me, and Manni stepped forward with a glass of water from the bedside. Liza drank some and calmed down, laying back flat on the pillow as she had been when I had entered the room.

Manni spoke next. "Liza and I were supposed to meet for dinner that evening, but she never showed." Manni set the glass down and brushed some of Liza's hair out of her eyes. "I searched for hours, and finally found her car run off the road. She was in a ditch, thrown away like garbage. She even had a needle in her arm. I thought she was dead. I wanted to call an ambulance, but the holes in her arms…" Manni shuddered a moment before collecting herself. "It didn't add up. Harry had some medical training before he got into accounting, so he came to help. Liza had never done drugs, and turning her in like this, she would lose her job. I couldn't let that happen."

"They tried to make it look like I'd done drugs before," Liza piped up again. She turned over her arm, exposing the inside. Needle marks ran up and down the skin, but they all looked fresh.

"Harry and I brought her and her car here, and we've been watching over her ever since."

"How am I supposed to call the cops on a senator? What would happen? He'd get a fine and a slap on the wrist for the assault charge, maybe, but my life would be ruined." Liza's sudden burst of energy dropped out from under her again. "It seems like it already is. I'm trapped here."

Now, more than ever, I felt the need to bring the senator to justice for his crimes. What he had done to this young woman was unforgivable.

"I'll make sure he'll pay for this. I promise." I stepped forward and clasped Liza's hand, the only way I knew to reassure her of my sincerity.

"Please," Manni begged, looking up from her sister's side. "See that you do."

I nodded and went back to my camera, stopped the recording and switched it off. "One more thing, and you don't have to if you don't want to."

"What is it?" Manni asked.

I looked Liza in the eye, sorry for what I had to say next. "Let Officer Ratledge arrest you."

Liza's "What?" was nearly drowned out by Manni's "Absolutely not!"

I put my hands up, trying to calm the sudden rise in emotion. "It's only for your protection. I found you here. It's only a matter of time before the senator's men will, too. It'd protect your sister and brother-in-law as well. Believe me, these people are not concerned about collateral damage. The cops can protect you, though. They're obligated to defend whistleblowers. You'd be safest with them."

"If there's one thing that would completely destroy my life, it'd be an arrest," Liza said. "I refuse to let him win."

I disagreed, but could hardly blame Liza for her decision. "Okay," I complied. "I have what I came for. But if you do change your mind, call Officer Ratledge. He'll protect you."

"Thank you," Liza said, understanding more than her sister did. "I'll keep that in mind."

"And feel free to call me at any time," I said, stepping toward the door.

"Anna?" Liza asked.

I turned back. "Yes?"

"Get this bastard for me."

I smiled at her fiery spirit. "I will."

8

Black sat, crouched in his corner, staring across the room at the corpse of the man he had killed. He had killed before, but never like this. It was always when he had no other choice. Back then, he had been able to leave before the body hit the ground. Never had he beaten a helpless man to a pulp, especially out of anger. Then, to make it all worse, Black couldn't keep from staring at his work, sitting there on the floor. The blood was already beginning to turn into tints of brown, and Black was powerless to remove himself or the mess.

Once the adrenaline had worn off, the real fallout from his injuries sustained during the fight reared its ugly head. His collar bone hurt the worst by far. He could move his arm, but not without excruciating pain. Even his breathing caused spider webs of agony across his upper body. His eye was starting to swell, too, and the blood behind his ear was starting to crust. It had bled for a full minute before stopping on its own. Black's fists, arms, and throat all ached as well, but not nearly to the extent of the rest of it.

He should move the body. Where to? There was nowhere. Maybe flip it over, so Black didn't have to see the face. Not that there was much face left to see. What hadn't been pounded flat was coated in blood, once ruby red, now dark as garnet and turning brown. No. Somehow, touching the body made it worse, even in concept. Real. Black wished he could close his eyes and be back at the office building or even at his house. Anywhere but where he was.

So, alone Black sat, with nothing but the corpse of a faceless man and that continuous buzz to keep him company.

The topography of the city made for advantages and disadvantages in each direction for somewhere to set up a secret government operation. Cyan couldn't narrow it down without seeing each location for himself. Mountains to the north would hide an underground facility. Plains to the east. Plenty of room to operate and establish a reason for traffic, such as setting up a veterinary hospital or something similar there.

There was also the sibling city to the south, with lots of buildings and traffic and two freeways from Cyan's current location to explore. Then to the west was a deep forest, capable of hiding anything under the cover of trees.

Without more information, which Scarlett had gone to seek, it was a coin toss. Cyan was about ready to pick one at random when Green called.

"What news?" Cyan asked.

"Not to the south," Green said. "I just watched him and Scarlett leave and they didn't take the south ramp." They could have gone any other direction from there, though.

"That's helpful, thank you. Interested in helping me scout tonight?"

"I'm on security duty." Right. Green was a guard for a freelance security business in town, and couldn't join Cyan on Sunday nights.

"Okay."

"Tell you what – I'm gonna stick around here until my shift starts. I'll let you know if things change."

"I appreciate it." Cyan hung up the phone and held it for a moment, thinking. It was at times like this he really needed to call on Black. He had a great focus for this sort of thing. Plus, Cyan had no real combat skills when it came to a fight. Cyan was just pretty good at talking and avoiding punches overall. He had attended Karate camp when he was in middle school, but couldn't really remember anything useful.

He knew going alone, after what happened to Black, was not a smart idea. Then again, what choice did he have? Limey? Cyan was better off alone.

He informed Silver of his plans and that he would check in after he stopped by each location. The last thing they needed was for another of their people to disappear.

It was on his second stop, to the eastern direction, that he got his first clue. He parked across the street from a vet's office and watched. There was a fleet of black vehicles in the parking lot which had caught his eye. Not outright criminal, but suspicious enough for Cyan to stop.

Cyan dug through the glove box for a snack as he watched. It was nearly dinner time. Granola bar. Close enough.

The only traffic in and out of the building had pet carriers. Either Cyan was wrong and this was just a vet's office, or they were using the pet carriers in some way to transport equipment.

After about ten minutes of watching and munching, a car pulled over to his side of the gravel shoulder. Had he been spotted? Cyan got out of his car, ready to assess the situation and talk his way out, if need be. To his surprise, Scarlett emerged from the driver's side of the car and slammed the door, as if in anger.

"Jack!" she shouted. She swore at him while another man, one Cyan had never seen before, stepped out of the car. She must be using Cyan as a cover somehow. "Are you stalking me now too, Jack?"

"I'm so sorry, please." Cyan assumed a weak posture, hoping to learn more about the story she was concocting and figure out what her plan was. "I'll never do it again."

"Uh huh, that's what you said last time." Jilted lover? Scarlett reached Cyan and slapped. Hard. What did she want from him? Her verbal attacks didn't end there, either, going on at length about his mother.

"Is this punk bothering you?" her passenger and their audience said. He was clearly all brawn and no brains. If he was following her, as she accused, why on earth would Cyan have gotten here first?

"First, he's reading my texts. Now, he's following me!"

Cyan spoke up, hoping to glean more about the situation. "I'm sorry, babe. It's because I love you."

Scarlett's flurry of motion suddenly stilled and she watched him, biting her lip. Man, she was really attractive when she wanted to be. "You... you love me?"

"Of course. I always have. Please forgive me." Forgiveness for what, Cyan still wasn't clear, but he didn't need to be. Reading her texts and following her, apparently.

"I love you too!" Scarlett launched at him again, this time to wrap her arms around Cyan's neck in a half hug. Then, to his surprise, she sprang up and kissed him. She took her time with the kiss, too. Okay then.

Cyan enjoyed it more than he cared to confess.

"Sorry, loser," Scarlett said after she finally backed away for a breath, turning to face the man she had arrived with but keeping one arm around Cyan's neck. "You're on your own tonight."

The man stared, appearing as dumbfounded as Cyan felt, as Cyan and Scarlett hopped back into his car and sped away, back toward the center of town.

Scarlett stared straight ahead, watching the road go by as Cyan drove. Normally she preferred to drive, but Cyan was the exception. He was the only one who didn't annoy or terrify her. She had always been a terrible back seat driver, she suspected.

"You know, I don't appreciate you talking about my mother that way," Cyan said, breaking the silence and palpable awkwardness. She had said some pretty crude things back there.

Scarlett laughed. "Sorry, 'babe'," she shot back, teasing.

"Well, how was I supposed to know what you had told him your name was?"

"It worked. I just have to make fun of you when I get the chance." Scarlett broke eye contact with the side of the road to look at him. He was still flushed, ever since she had kissed him.

"Are we going to talk about the – "

"Nope," Scarlett interrupted. The sooner they both forgot about the kiss, the better. "They live on base, so it is on this side of town," Scarlett recited, going back to watching the road. She didn't want to make him feel too self-conscious. "I saw you and had to bail before we got back." She would have slept with the lummox of a man, if it came to that, but was glad for the excuse to escape.

"That's it?"

"Of course not." She reached into her bra and pulled out an ID card she had found in the man's car.

Cyan took it from her and looked back and forth from it to the road before handing it back. "That's more like it."

"Also, Black's alive."

"Why didn't you start there?" Cyan's excitement was visible.

Scarlett shrugged. "There's a woman watching over him. Natasha Markham. She's in charge of Lewitt's Containment Division."

"Containment." Cyan's enthusiasm turned to disgust, visible in the slight downturn of his lips and the furrowing of his eyebrows. Scarlett could hardly blame him.

"It's a name. It'll give Anna something to work on." Scarlett didn't quite know how to feel about another woman's presence in her territory, but she was helpful and posed no real threat to Scarlett and her operations. Live and let live, she supposed.

"She's going by White now," Cyan informed her.

"Makes no difference to me," Scarlett responded.

I was busy copying the raw footage of the interview to the drives that held the first video I had captured of the senator when Cyan entered the room. Liza's story changed the game from assault to attempted murder, at least when it came to evidence I had collected. If I could find out more about Brian's fate, then perhaps murder charges would be added, too.

Cyan waited politely for my attention before saying anything. "We have the name of Black's captor," he informed me as I turned to him.

Black was alive, then! I barely knew the man, but was sincerely relieved to hear the news. "What can I do to help?"

"You've proven useful in finding people. We're working on where, but we could use a little more about who."

I pulled out my little notepad to write down the details. "Shoot," I said, pen ready.

"Natasha Markham."

A female? "Is that the notorious blonde?" I asked. Finally a name to the face.

"We're hoping you can confirm that. She's working under Senator Lewitt, and likely the cause of all this damage. If we take her out, we're taking the fangs from the viper, so to speak."

I liked the sound of that. Without fear of repercussion from this woman, exposure of the senator's crimes would be swift and crippling to his career. Part of me wanted to go further, to cripple *him*, but that was vengeance, not justice.

"Do we have anything else?" I asked. My notepad just read the name, Senator Lewitt, and blonde followed by a question mark.

"Our best operative is looking into it," Cyan said, pointing a pen in my direction and evidently referring to me.

"I'll try not to let you down," I responded, smiling. "Oh, take a look at this when you get the chance." I tossed one of the flash drives that already held the interview to him. He caught it easily.

Cyan eyed me questioningly. "I've already seen the clip."

"And now it also contains the interview with the woman the senator hit."

Cyan looked impressed, and I couldn't help but beam. "Keep up the good work, White." He smiled and left, tossing the flash drive in the air and catching it as he left.

I turned my attention to my computer just as the video finished copying onto another drive. I could accomplish both tasks - new and old - at the same time.

Natasha Markham sat in the observation room, only a window separating herself and Black. She felt no fear from her prisoner, and even rather enjoyed being in there with him. But he wasn't where she wanted him: in complete submission to her.

Not yet.

He was breaking, she had no doubt. They always broke in the end. Black was proving hardier than the others, though. The corpse still lay in the room with him. The man had once been in Black's position, though not nearly so composed by this point. He was ready, eager, even, to obey her. In the end, though, he had failed her. She made sure he paid the price.

Natasha reached over and turned the lights in the room off, curious how Black would respond. She still watched him through screens displaying thermal signatures. Black's shape read yellow and orange through his upper body, a clear sign of anxiety and anger, but his lower half read as a cooler blue, indicating surprise or, if sustained, shame. The body on the other side of the room still read as a faint outline. The room was now down to a cool 58 degrees Fahrenheit and the sensors had adjusted accordingly.

She watched with interest, elbows on the cool countertop and hands in fists under her chin. Everyone reacted differently at this point.

Black's first reaction was to look up. Then he stood, clearly alert and ready for something, though she knew nothing would come. Times like this revealed a lot about who she was dealing with and what they wanted. The colors on the display shifted to show suspicion. About thirty seconds went by in near absolute stillness.

Then, just when Black threatened to bore Natasha, he moved. At first, it looked like he was stretching, then she realized he was taking his shirt off, though slowly because of his injuries. He turned away from the window and sensors, though she wouldn't be able to see anything even if he were facing the window. He stilled again for a moment and his colors changed to echo relief. Why?

Natasha nodded slightly as she realized he was using the restroom. Everyone had a different reaction to the darkness, and to Black it meant privacy. Some had panicked, while others had simply wept at their isolation. One had even taken it as a sign to go to sleep. Black was special, though. The darkness was a time to move, to be productive by himself. In this instance, in the most primal of ways.

After he finished, Black then threw the shirt, visibly warm from urine, across the room. Natasha wasn't sure if he was aiming for the body, but it landed perfectly in the corner next to the door and far from him. If that was his goal, it was remarkable aim for one who had no visual references. Natasha would love to see him fight in the dark some time. Not without pain relievers, though, with his arm in the state it was in. She could remedy that easily enough with a few pills.

Again Black did something unexpected. Natasha thought he would return to his crouch in the corner, but instead he walked halfway down the wall to the bowls that held the water and a place for food. He used his right hand to scoop the water to his face, not going down to the bowl. He did nothing more than drink the water, either choosing not to waste it or in an effort to keep warm by not soaking himself while he sat in the cold room. His aim was precise, however, never fumbling around to find the bowl.

The water. That was her way in. She could drug the water with medications. However, making him depend on them, like some common street addiction, felt beneath her pet project somehow. She could, however, make him dependent on *her* for relief.

Natasha smiled as she left the room, flicking the light back on and turning up the buzz just two decibels. There was a plan in place, and she was looking forward to executing it.

Next, however, she had someone else to visit. He went by Monday, and had been in isolation for months. He had shared very little with her, even under the effects of her toolkit. This time he had gone two weeks without any human contact, and she hoped even hearing a voice might make him eager to talk to her now.

The night passed relatively unproductively. Cyan had gone home in his black Camaro. It was too signature to use to scout again, so he would have to wait for Green and use his car tomorrow.

His estate was massive, purchased by his father when Cyan was too young to remember anything else.

Someone took Cyan's coat as his sister came running down the stairs to greet him.

"I got an A on my project!" she announced without preamble. She was fourteen, and the light of his life. If ever Cyan lost track of why he did what he did with the organization, just Breanne's smile was enough to remind him.

"That's great!" he said, hugging her with both arms. He had helped with her project: a Rube-Goldberg machine that raised a flag. They had fun building it together, despite their age difference.

If anything ever happened to her, Cyan didn't know what he'd do. Anger boiled inside him just at the thought.

"What?" Breanne asked, detecting his shift in mood and pulling away.

"Nothing. Any more projects I can help with?"

"Just a history paper." She stuck out her tongue. She was more of a science person, like their dad. Cyan recalled they had been working through the colonial period in America the last time he had spoken with her. It had not been a topic of interest when he was her age, but now, working with the organization, Cyan was especially intrigued by the original concepts behind the Constitution. The government these days, it seemed to Cyan, was only a hollow shell of what it had been at that point in history.

"Let me see if we can make it interesting."

Breanne lit up at Cyan's offer to help, and they walked up the stairs together as she explained the assignment. Cyan couldn't help but smile. Life was good.

Monday

9

I spent the night at the office building again. It took some asking around before I could find a shower, though. Finally Limey told me he frequented the one in the gym down the block. I gave it a shot, but was forced back into my dirty jeans and t-shirt I had worn since the incident at my apartment.

To my surprise, Scarlett was waiting for me when I got back.

"What can I do for you?" I asked. I still didn't quite know what to make of her. She had mostly ignored me since I arrived. I supposed that was logical, since, if you could sort people here by uses, we were in separate divisions. She was definitely more field work and I more in data collection and intelligence.

"I have a gift for you," Scarlett said, leading me into the room where I had slept again. I tried not to let my suspicion show. Somehow, it felt like she was the cheerleader and I the band geek. "Okay," Scarlett said once we were isolated. "Promise not to be offended?"

I'm sure my confusion was evident. I had made no attempt to hide it. "I can't guarantee that, but I'll try," I said honestly.

"That outfit doesn't suit you at all."

"It's not what I normally wear," I confessed, looking down. My shirt was crumpled from sleeping in it for two nights straight and wet spots still appeared on my shoulder from my hair. I knew my back was darkened by water, too, as my hair was still a long way from being dry.

When I looked up, Scarlett had produced a rather nice white blouse and a charcoal pencil skirt to go with it. "Don't worry, I have shoes for you, too." That was definitely not my first thought, but her statement told me something about the woman across from me. She shoved the outfit into my hands and turned around, conjuring fashionable but professional heels that matched the skirt perfectly.

"Thank you," I said, sincerely grateful for her generosity.

"Don't worry about it." Scarlett smiled at me. "Try it on! I want to make sure they fit."

I changed out of the grungy clothes into the new outfit. That, combined with the shower, and I felt almost like a new person.

"Isn't that better?" she asked.

I had to agree. "Very much so. Thank you." I watched her smile and skip past me. "Scarlett?" I asked, stopping her with my words.

"Yes?"

"Why did you do this?"

Scarlett shrugged and smiled winningly at me. "I didn't like your old outfit. You've a much prettier figure than those jeans show off." The first sentence struck me strangely. It wasn't exactly a lie, but maybe not the real reason behind her act of kindness. That instinct – my internal lie detector – was helpful at times, but others it led to more confusion than it was worth. I didn't understand her motives, but Scarlett was making an effort to be kind to me, and I could appreciate that.

I smiled back – I had to agree with her statement – and followed her out. I had made a friend here.

Green greeted us in the hallway. "Hurry up, you two. Whole team meeting."

I stepped a little faster to catch up and follow him.

Everyone had gathered in the main conference room, save for Green, Scarlett, and myself. I slipped into the closest chair I could find to make as little noise as possible. Even Silver was there, to my surprise. Hadn't I just seen him in the hall on my way over? Apparently not. Every seat, save one, was full. That one stood as a reminder that we had a man still missing. There were also four members in the room I had not yet met, sitting on the other side of Saturday.

"Alright," Saturday said, standing. He could have easily been a used car salesman. For all I knew, he was one. But inside these walls, he was their leader. Our leader. "First, I'd like to introduce White, the newest member of our organization."

A smattering of applause sprinkled through the small group. I had no idea why they applauded me. Most of them knew already.

"Most of you have heard that we have a member who is not here this morning. Black has been captured by them and has been unable to make free contact since he left here the night before last. There's a lot of information out there, and I wanted to make sure we were all on the same page moving forward." Saturday paused, looking over the group of people. "He may not have been the warmest member of our crew, but make no mistake – he is very dear to us." To Saturday more than most, I could see. What was the story there? "Cyan? Would you like to give us the timeline?"

Saturday sat as Cyan stood. "Black was abducted from his home in the early morning hours Sunday. Orange has gone to his place and confirmed they used non-lethal means." One of the men I didn't know, the one seated between Saturday and Limey, nodded. He must be Orange. He had an awkward but simultaneously comfortable posture about him. The question of how he got his name passed through my mind, but I rejected it in favor of listening to Cyan. "I spoke to him yesterday morning. He made it clear that he was being held against his will. Other than that, it's been all guess work.

It seems they want him alive for the time being, but to what end, we have no idea. Scarlett, want to tell us about where?"

Scarlett stood, gracefully as always, and immediately commanded the attention of everyone in the room. "We've narrowed it down to one of three buildings, all about ten miles east of the city. This conclusion came from clues of this conversation with Black, mostly." She indicated to Cyan, who – from what I understood – had recorded the conversation and spearheaded their study into Black's words.

Limey waved his hand, getting Scarlett's attention and permission to speak. "I –" Limey stammered. Why was he nervous? The next sentence came out in a rush, as if he were trying to get the moment over as quickly as possible. "I've analyzed the signal, and I think he was underground at the time of the conversation." He dropped his head, and I realized he was just intimidated. The poor guy spent all his time on a computer, and likely didn't do much speaking publicly. He flushed a little when he looked back up, and I realized it was because Scarlett was smiling at him. I smiled at Limey too, but only to encourage him and show appreciation for gathering the courage to share what he knew.

Scarlett relieved him. "Thank you. We also have a key card, which Limey has agreed to analyze." The Brit flushed even deeper red and kept his head down. "Cyan and I hope to figure out which building by the end of today." She sat, and Cyan countered her, standing again.

"I think I'll have Green help you there, actually," Cyan said. I saw Green bow his head, neck muscles bulging as he agreed to the task. "Black also indicated in the conversation that he only had one captor that spoke to him, at least. White, would you like to tell us what you've learned about her?"

Surprised, I stood, clasping my hands. It was a habit I had picked up when I first started reporting outside of college. Apparently I moved my hands too much when giving a report, and I refused to take a script with me. If I didn't know the story by heart, I didn't understand it all enough to report it.

"Natasha Markham. Ph.D. in Biochemistry from San Jose State University. She started working for Senator Lewitt soon after. She specializes in mind-altering drugs." How much should I tell? Most of what I had learned was irrelevant. "Since she was hired, there's been about a 25-percent increase in accidental deaths among Senator Lewitt's enemies. Many of those have been drug related, either prescription or street. Wherever Senator Lewitt travels, Markham's work seems to follow." What next?

"What about family?" Saturday asked from his seat. He must have noticed my hesitation.

Thankfully I had researched the answer to his question already. "Foster parents are both dead. He had a heart attack in his sleep and she mixed the wrong kind of drugs with alcohol a month later. It appeared there was a foster brother in the picture at one point, too, but his Facebook profile says he's an only child, so I'm not quite clear there. Markham also never had a pet last more than a year when she was young."

I couldn't think of anything else to share, so I sat again. Fortunately Cyan saved me from leaving the room in an awful silence. "Moving forward," Cyan said, standing again. "We've agreed with Black that we will come for him tomorrow. As far as we know, they are unaware of this fact, and that is our only advantage. I expect, if Black is even conscious when we find him, he will not be in any state to help. Green will be in charge of the operation, so go to him if you'd like to contribute somehow or happen to learn anything relevant."

Saturday stood as Cyan sat, though I couldn't think of anything else that needed to be addressed.

"One last reminder: please, please, please check in and out with Silver. I don't want any harm to come to another of you. Each of you is vital to this operation. Thank you."

And like that, we were dismissed. I had to say, it was one of the least bureaucratic and most efficient meetings I had attended in my lifetime.

Black had lost any sense of time. The two minutes or so during which the lights had been turned off had fooled him into thinking they would grant him darkness at night, but they didn't. The buzzing and cold, combined with the brightness, prevented more than an hour of sleep total. For all he knew, it could have been an afternoon nap or a midnight snooze. The only reason he deduced it had been an hour is that at this temperature, he knew his body would only let him sleep on the cold, hard ground for that long at maximum. Combined with his shoulder, all hope for more was lost.

He needed the sleep, too. He hadn't eaten since Saturday night. In optimal outer conditions, the hunger would not have bothered him in the least. Here, however, his body needed the nutrients to heal not only his collar bone, but his bruised knuckles and swollen eye, too. That, and food often served as a substitute for sleep, in the way his body accounted for things.

Black's eye felt almost back to normal, though. He could open it fully with only a little soreness. He had only the window to see how it looked, but minus a little bruising under the eye, everything appeared the same as always.

His collar bone was another story. Fortunately, if he overlooked a little swelling in the area, his shoulder looked normal. The arm attached to it, however, hung limply by his side. He could move it, but the dull ache swelled to a throb whenever he tried. Even turning his wrist over sent new spasms of pain. Now shirtless, it was easy to see in the

window his arm was definitely less useful and more...
wounded was the only way he could think to describe it.

Black sat back in his corner, but this time pressed his
shoulder gently against the cold brushed steel. The
temperature difference was both shocking and comforting. He
felt now, more than ever, like a caged animal. Trapped with
the corpse of a man and the stench of his own urine; confined
to drinking out of a dog bowl.

This was exactly what Mother wanted.

As if the mere thought had conjured her, Black heard
the door click and open. The corpse still rested against it and
flopped into the hallway beyond as the door gave way.
Mother appeared, casually stepping over the man, and again
the buzzing faded, enough so that Black could think. He even
found himself welcoming the click of Mother's heels.

"Hello again, my dear," she said as she approached
him.

Black pulled his knees up to his chest, aware this was
the first time she had seen him, at least not through the
window, shirtless. He looked at her, but refused to speak.

"Come now, don't be shy. Stand up." She offered her
right hand to his left, but there was no way he would have
taken it even if he could put any weight on that side.

Black shook his head and looked anywhere else. The
corpse was disappearing through the doorway, presumably
being dragged by some force beyond.

"Would it make you more comfortable if I took my
shirt off, too?" No, it would not. Black didn't speak though,
and Mother removed her blouse.

Her skin rippled with goose bumps. So the cold
wasn't only in his imagination. She knelt in his line of sight,
still sporting a black bra, then sat next to him on his left side.
A flash of rebellion passed through Black's mind, arm cleanly
landing in her throat and breaking her windpipe. The fantasy
disappeared as quickly as it came.

"I'm hungry," she said suddenly. "Are you hungry?"

Black nodded, hating himself for answering her. But how else was he going to get food? He needed it if he was going to be able to fight this. Fight her. What an odd predicament he found himself in.

Only until they came to rescue him. When? Tomorrow or the next day. How long had he been in there? Every part of him wanted to ask, but he refused.

After watching him for a moment, Mother stood again and walked out of the room, leaving her blouse crumpled loosely where she sat, and pausing only to pick up the thus-far empty food bowl. The food must have been right outside the door, because she returned moments later with the dog bowl she had picked up and a bowl meant for humans in the other hand, the latter boasting some sort of eating utensil.

"Here you go," she cooed, handing him the dog bowl. Black dropped his knees and put it on his lap. Mother sat too, this time across from him and in his line of sight. "Bon appétit."

Good appetite. That he had.

The bowl was filled with some sort of chocolate cereal. The milk underneath exposed itself as the metal shifted in his hand. Breakfast. That meant it must be morning in the world beyond. Probably not Tuesday morning yet, so that meant it was only Monday. Unless she was messing with him, which was most likely.

Black filtered the brown chocolate-flavored balls through his fingers as he ate, finishing all he could before bringing the bowl to his mouth and drinking out of it as if it were the largest, shallowest mug on the planet. This was what he was condemned to now. Black almost wished he hadn't spoken to Cyan and requested rescue. Then he could do something brash and Mother would be forced to kill him. Then it'd all be over.

After the meeting, I chased Saturday down. He chatted with Cyan in the room I had met him in yesterday, so I waited outside. After about half an hour, Cyan left, nodding to me as he crossed the threshold into the hallway. He knew I was there, waiting. Cyan didn't miss a thing.

"Come in, please, White," came the voice from inside the room. Neither, apparently, did Saturday.

I stepped into the room and shook his hand again, smiling and sitting in the same chair I had yesterday.

"Thank you for your research and report today. It was very informative."

"It's what I do," I said, smiling back. "Thank you."

"That's not why you waited outside my door, though." Saturday peered at me over his glasses. "You're here to ask about Black, aren't you?"

I couldn't help the surprise on my face. How did he know that? "I am," I answered, grateful I didn't have to find a way to breach the subject myself.

"Why?"

"The more I know about him, the more help I can be in rescuing him. He's something of a mystery to me still." All I had said was true, but it wasn't the whole truth. The man intrigued me. He seemed intellectual at heart but more than physically competent. He seemed a contradiction, but so very self-controlled and put together.

Saturday leaned back in his chair, thinking. "You are probably more capable in guessing his current situation than I." My stomach turned at the thought of what Black could be experiencing in the clutches of that woman.

I felt myself click into reporter mode as I leaned forward and asked my question, steering the conversation in the direction I wished it to go. "How did you meet him?"

Saturday pursed his lips, thinking before answering. "In short, his brother was the one we called Monday, a close friend of mine. I first met Black when I joined Monday for his coming home party."

"From the Air Force?" I asked, more to make sure the information I had already gleaned about the man was accurate.

"Yes. Black is an honorable man. Once you have his loyalty, it takes a lot to break it. But once it's gone, there is no recovering it." Saturday paused, clearly choosing his words with care.

"What is it? You can be honest with me." I spoke sincerely, trying to put the man at ease.

Saturday nodded. "Don't be too quick to judge Black for what I have to say next." He waited for my nod before continuing. "Rarely do we pursue people to join our organization, but we wanted Black. He's intelligent and incredibly skilled, and it wouldn't take long before he realized the fallacy in blind obedience to the government. I say obedience, not trust, with intention. What we didn't count on was his overwhelming sense of loyalty. At this point in his life, he had spent eight years with the government and two weeks with his brother.

"Black turned Monday in. He reported me, and the others he had met in our group. It was because of his actions the government even knows about our organization's existence now."

I was mortified. Not only because of Black's actions then, but because I knew the organization had now fully accepted Black as a member.

"Two of our number were arrested that day, and another two killed in the fight," Saturday continued. "Monday and Friday were those arrested. Black did feel guilty about what he did. I think the government broke his trust with them somehow, but Black has never told me outright. He went back to his brother to explain, not necessarily to apologize for his actions. That's when Black fully realized his mistake. The government 'misfiled' Monday's paperwork," Saturday raised his hand to make air quotes around "misfiled," then continued, "and Monday was gone. The government killed him.

"Black found Tuesday and explained everything. Tuesday naturally treated him with suspicion. He didn't want the man he saw as a traitor anywhere near the organization, understandably. So I let Black follow me here. He's been a loyal and helpful member ever since. At first, I think he was trying to repay us for what he had done, but now I know he truly believes in our cause. He knows more deeply than most exactly what the government is capable of. Now, I fear, firsthand."

One element of the story stuck out in my mind. "Did you ever see Monday's body?" I asked. I needed proof if I were to believe it. Maybe not to see it myself, but to know that there was evidence out there.

Saturday smiled at my question. "Eternally the optimist, aren't you? That's what I like about having you here. To answer your question, no. The government isn't so careless."

"So there's a chance he could be alive somewhere?" I persisted.

"I wish that were so." Sadness traced his features, and I wanted to do what I could to make the joy return. Finding the truth, and his friend, would do just that. But how?

Silence filled the room. We both sat back in our chairs, pondering the horrors of what had been done, and what was being done to Black now.

10

Scarlett joined Green at the billiards parlor again. She often went with him, into the lion's den, so to speak. It gave her a thrill, operating right under their noses like this. The government knew only their code names by monitoring their communications. That couldn't be helped. But so long as the disconnect remained between their code names and their real ones, they were safe.

There was a pool table in the corner that always had a RESERVED placard on it and a game in progress. Most days the balls shifted, almost as if of their own accord. She liked to think of it as night gremlins playing while everybody else slept. Though, with the people who frequented this establishment, they'd probably have to be morning gremlins.

In reality, however, gremlins had nothing to do with it. This particular pool table held the communications to and from the government about Scarlett's organization. Green had once explained to her how to read it. The different balls on the table represented different members of the organization. She was the seven ball, Blue the two, and so on.

Today, however, something was different. Today, for the first time, Scarlett saw people playing at the table. Green had disappeared, presumably to the restroom, when a young man and one who could have passed for his father grabbed a couple of cues and re-racked for a fresh game. Watching them, one would think they were playing by a completely different set of rules.

Neither spoke as the young man quickly dropped several balls, none of which had any correlation to the organization, at least not to Scarlett's knowledge. There was no purple in the organization, so the four was quickly dropped. The younger man then knocked the black one right on the edge of a pocket and stepped back, letting the older man, likely the superior officer, step in and play. That made sense – Black was in their clutches and close to death. The closer the balls were to the pocket, the more danger they were in. Each pocket was also associated with a government agent, if Green was to be believed.

As she watched, Scarlett was pleased to see her seven stay close to the center of the table. She wasn't seen as much of a threat. Not one to be dealt with now, at least. The green sphere was put closer to a pocket before the older man knocked it away, back to the center. Interesting. Without a word, the two were having an argument about who to target next.

Finally, the older man made a move that made Scarlett sit upright in her seat. Without aiming at any particular colored ball, he shot the cue ball – the white one – into a pocket.

They were targeting White? How did they know she even existed? She had only been introduced to the organization an hour ago, maybe an hour and a half, tops.

Green arrived back, and must have noticed Scarlett's posture. "What is it?" he asked, somewhere between bored and concerned.

"Nothing," she responded casually, but indicated with her eyes toward the pool table. The pair had replaced the RESERVED sign and were putting away their cues.

She looked back at Green, watching him comprehend the status of the table. "They're targeting White?" he said suddenly, whispering.

Scarlett dropped her volume to match his. "They know White exists."

His eyes grew big as he came to the same conclusion Scarlett had. Then, suddenly, he grabbed his jacket and left money on the bar counter for his drink. "I'm going to follow them," he said as the door clinked and the men exited. "Call Saturday. Tell him we have a mole."

Cyan was with Saturday when he got the phone call. Normally their leader was the picture of calm composure, but as he spoke with whomever it was on the other side, he sat erect, then stood, then started pacing the room. It disturbed Cyan just to see Saturday so moved.

"That's not possible," Saturday said for the fourth time.

Cyan caught Saturday's eye, silently requesting he put the phone on speaker so Cyan could hear too. Perhaps he could help?

Saturday understood his request, but didn't comply. What on earth could it be that he couldn't share with him? He was entitled to his personal life, but it was out of character for him to blatantly refuse to share information. It opposed everything the organization stood for.

Maybe he should leave. Clearly he wasn't welcome. As he reached the door, Saturday finally addressed him, but not to stop his departure. "Cyan, send White back in." All politeness was gone from his voice.

Cyan nodded and exited. What was it that White could know and he couldn't? The idea disturbed Cyan to the core. He found White with a laptop in the same room as Limey, though Limey was in the corner with headphones on in his usual hunched-over posture.

"Cyan!" White spotted him excitedly. "I found a useful piece of insight here." She prodded the screen, which boasted a YouTube video. "It's a speech Markham gave while at school."

He leaned over her shoulder and watched as she played the video. It was amateur, likely filmed with a cell phone, but the audio was clear.

"I intend to prove that you can change a person – who they are at their core – by changing body chemistry. Hormone treatments are already commonly used for that purpose. Adderall for those who have no ability to focus. But what about more? I propose that you can not only use chemicals to make one less or more aggressive, but even go so far as to change how they see the world. With the right ingredients, even a love potion, as it were, would not be out of reach. With the right chemicals, and we as a species are nothing but chemicals, you could customize any person to become anything they want to be."

White hit pause and let the words freeze the air. For a moment, Cyan forgot why he was there. This video blatantly laid out all their fears as to what Markham was doing to Black, perhaps even at that particular moment.

Cyan shook his head, remembering his purpose. "Good to know, thank you. Saturday needs you now, though."

White raised an eyebrow questioningly. "Now? I just spoke to him."

"I know."

"What about?" she asked. Cyan watched her gather her things and shut down the laptop.

"I've no idea." That bothered him more than he cared to admit.

White shrugged and thanked him, making sure to grab her spiral binder that held all her notes as she left.

Cyan watched her go, a twinge of emotion rolling through him. It took him a moment to be honest enough with himself to identify it: jealousy. She was about to learn the secret Saturday was blatantly keeping from him.

"A mole?" I asked, confused. "How does that happen?"

"I have no idea." All composure in the man now seemed forced, as if Saturday was arguing with himself and I was just a witness.

"Why are you telling me?" I asked. As the newest member of the organization, it made more sense for me to be the last person Saturday gave the information to. "How do you know you can trust me?"

"You're the target."

"I've always been the target," I countered. That was how I got involved in the organization in the first place.

"White is the target, not just the reporter who filmed what she wasn't supposed to." How could they know my code name? Then my thoughts caught up with his as they connected the dots.

"Okay. Who do we know we can trust?" I said, writing down as many names as I knew in the organization. The sooner we got intentional with the research, the sooner we could reveal the truth.

"Everybody." Sadness crossed Saturday's face. "Or so I thought."

There was no chance Black could have revealed the secret while he was in there, I reasoned. The timeline didn't fit. I had gotten my name after he had gone into their custody.

"Who are the other four?" I asked. "The ones at the meeting this morning?"

Saturday quickly read my list before responding. "Orange." Right. I knew that one. I jotted it down. Each name was said with evident affection for the one it represented. "Orange is our clean-up man. He goes in after the scenes to make sure the public doesn't catch on or worse, get dragged into it. Red is our accountant. He's a magician with numbers. Limey – You've already got him. Our resident lawyer is Gold. Lavendar does much of our cooking. He can get into almost anywhere with his crème brulee. None of them could possibly be..." His voice trailed off as he paced.

"Unfortunately, someone is." I hated to contemplate it, but there it was. "Can we assume that it was someone who just learned my name?" I asked. This did, after all, happen just after I had been announced to the group as a whole.

"Unless the person was waiting to throw us off their scent. We can't assume that, no."

"Who all knows?" I asked, referring to the fact that we had a mole.

"You, Scarlett, Green, and myself." I could see the honesty plastered on his face, riddled with concern. I had always been good at detecting lies, and I could tell there was no dishonesty in that countenance.

"Not Cyan?" I asked, surprised. He was the one to come and get me, after all.

"Not yet." Saturday exhaled slowly. "He needs to be cleared soon. He will be helpful in the rest of your investigation."

"My investigation?"

"Yes. If I led it, I'd lose the trust of everyone until it's over, and I can't afford that, not now. Please, do this for me?"

"Absolutely." Investigative journalism indeed.

I stared at the list. Cyan first, if possible, then I wanted Blue next. He was used to reading people, right? He was the closest I had to an actual interrogator. The thought of the task ahead taxed my already worn emotions. Why couldn't everybody just be trustworthy? I knew I was naïve for thinking it, but things would just be so much easier.

Natasha left Black's room, satisfied with his progress. She would be able to craft him as she wished, it would just take longer than most. That was fine. The harder the metal, the better the steel. She'd heard at one point that the highest prized samurai swords were folded more than ten times before they would be satisfactory to use in war. Black was going to be her sword. She just had to hammer and fold him first.

Next on her to do list today was to approach Monday. Once she got the information about the organization from him, he would die. Natasha was sure he knew that, too. That was why he had held out so long. But she had a good feeling about today. Success with Black had put her in a good mood, as did the intel from her mole that the reporter was working directly with the organization. The fact they planned to strike tomorrow just sweetened the deal.

Natasha donned her blouse again as soon as she was out of sight of Black. She had enjoyed making him uncomfortable, but she needed to be all business with Monday.

Monday was kept in more of a cell than an interrogation room, such as Black's. This room wasn't more than twelve feet squared, but that was enough room for the toilet, cot, and a chair. Natasha thought about her approach as she walked up to the bars on the outer wall of his cell. The man didn't seem to notice her, though the line of sight was clear. He was fully clothed and sitting on the toilet instead of the chair or bed.

"Hello, Monday." The moment the words left her lips the man looked up. His eyes had dark circles around them, presumably from a lack of sleep. He had many scars all over his body, which shined faintly, like trophies in the cold light. Perhaps she would add to them again soon. "How are you today?"

"The usual," he responded. "Same old, same old." He stood, slowly for a man still younger than forty. "You haven't visited me in a while."

"Sorry about that." Natasha enjoyed their banter, unproductive as it was. "Why did you sit on the toilet when there are much better seats around?" She tried to make her question sound casual, but curious.

"I do my best thinking on the toilet," Monday explained. He stretched and flexed his still considerable muscle. Natasha assumed that the only way he could be this strong, maybe even stronger than when he first came into her custody, was that he exercised. "I've been writing a poem. *The caged bird's song moves, sunlight behind bars bears hope.* I can't think of a third line that suits it, though."

Haiku. Part of Natasha wondered if he had finally snapped. "*Freedom's beauty lies?*" she offered.

Monday nodded and hummed assent, turning his back on her, but did not say more.

"Can I bring you anything? Are you comfortable?"

"What do you want, Miss Markham?" he asked, carefully inspecting a corner of the blank ivory wall. She could see remnants of what must have once been convincing charm, even from his posture.

Natasha decided she would try a new tactic. "Does the name Humphrey Black mean anything to you?"

Monday spun quickly again to face her.

She had predicted a reaction from him – after all, Black was the man responsible for Monday's imprisonment – but not a reaction this strong. Natasha smiled. Perhaps today would bring progress after all.

"What have you done to him?" Monday asked. Concern tainted his voice, not revenge. Interesting.

"He's safe. We just had breakfast together, in fact."

"Did you poison him?"

"Not in the least. The milk had painkillers in it, that's all."

"Did he come of his own accord?"

"He ate of his own accord." Natasha watched Monday nod and start making his bed, though it was already straighter than hers was at that moment. "Do you want me to kill him?" she asked. She could only imagine she would want the man responsible for her imprisonment dead, were their positions switched.

"No." The answer came quickly and without hesitation.

"So that you can kill him yourself?" Was his response motivated by mercy or selfishness?

Monday smiled and leaned over, tucking the blanket over the cot. What did that mean? As always, Monday's responses were cryptic and laden with multiple meanings. Maybe progress wasn't going to happen today after all.

"You're not going to give me anything, are you?" Natasha asked, calm on the outside but frustration starting to boil within.

"You won't break him."

"I've already broken him." It was stretching the truth a little bit, but Monday couldn't know that.

"That man is the reason this whole operation will fail." Monday waved his hands around, indicating to the camera and the hard walls that surrounded three sides of him.

Natasha was highly aware of her emotions gripping her. She had to step away before they started to show. Therefore, she nodded curtly to Monday, a calm smile on her face, and started to walk away. She was almost to the door when his voice reached her again.

"Miss Markham?"

She paused, but didn't turn back to face him. She couldn't. Not without showing her hand.

"That man, whenever you cage him, will end you. Do you want to know how I know that? Because that man, Humphrey Louis Black, is my brother. And I guarantee you, he is great at destroying what he doesn't like."

The threat, or warning, didn't even faze her. The information, though, that was like striking gold! Not only could she use Black against Monday, but vice versa. A little research and she could finally learn Monday's real name.

She continued marching toward the door, no longer stifling anger but instead let loose the broadest of grins.

Green sat in his car alone. He had followed the man from the pool hall to a building east of town, just down the street from the veterinary office. He had pulled past the building on first sight, not wishing to draw too much attention. He had then doubled back and sat parked, on the same side of the street as the building, staring at the back of it.

A black chain link fence wrapped around the property filled with dry, tall grasses. The building sat at the very center, almost like a concrete yolk in the center of his breakfast. Cameras peppered the building as well, but Green had chosen this spot to park because of the large tree that blocked their view of him. One – no, two – men on patrol. The first, standing atop the building, was easy to spot. The second waded through the dry grass, staring down at something in his hand. Green got out of the car to get a better look, careful to close the door silently. Both men wore all black. Standard-issue vests and guns.

A sudden stillness interrupted Green's thoughts. The man on top of the building had stopped moving. Had he been spotted? Green looked to the one on the ground right as that man, as large and muscular as Green, pulled his gun. Green had maybe half a second to decide how to react. The guard would fire on him, Green knew that. Firing back would take time. His gun was on the passenger seat and he didn't want to draw unwanted attention with return fire. Green's army knife was on his hip, as always, and the blade was his preferred weapon for this sort of scenario, when stealth was required.

Green dropped backward, on the far side of the car from the man firing, the same instant he saw the muzzle flash.

He heard the bullet fly by his left ear as he threw his weight down. Ha! He had actually dodged a bullet! More or less. His ear felt a sting a moment later. The bullet had not pierced him, but had been so close that it had burned part of his ear lobe.

He sprawled himself out on the ground, face up, as if he had been struck. He lay there for not more than ten seconds before the man who had fired on him approached the car from the passenger side and around the hood.

"I'm checking now," he said into the handheld part of his radio fastened to his shoulder. The voice was gruff and curt. Checking to make sure he had killed Green, no doubt. Eyes closed, Green heard the man crouch by his left side and felt him grab his left wrist. This was his chance. Green wrapped his left hand around his opponent's wrist and pulled. The tug helped Green get up while simultaneously bringing the man's face to Green's right fist. The punch landed beautifully and sent the guard back into the wheel of the car. The man looked remarkably like Green, and he knew they would be well-matched in a fight, at least physically.

The agent wrested his hand away and pulled his gun back out from his hip. Green had the upper hand now, though, and slammed his open palm into the side of the Glock. He closed his hand around it, holding the slide in place. The gun might still fire, but only one round as the casing would get jammed. Green got his feet under him then and pulled at the gun, but the agent refused to let it go. Simultaneously, as each side tugged for control of the gun, they inadvertently helped each other stand the rest of the way up.

Green torqued the right side of his body back, still clutching the slide of the gun with his left hand, and released the built up tension, slamming his right into the gun. He was rewarded with a small but distinct crunch as the man's thumb broke against the handle of the weapon.

The force of the slam sent the Glock flying, skidding to a halt three quarters of the way across the road. Too far for either of them to reach without giving the other a chance to land a free punch or two.

While Green was still deciding to let the gun go, the agent lifted his leg for a kick. Seeing it well enough in advance, Green lifted his left knee in order to check it, chin down and fists up for protection of his core. Green felt the kick land harmlessly and stepped in with his left, clocking the guy with his right just above the eye. He could have gone for nearly anywhere, but the Kevlar his opponent wore made the head a more desirable target.

The agent spun satisfactorily, a gash over his eyebrow. The man glared at him, but Green was in no mood to stop. He was on a roll now. His left fist came back, aiming for the floating rib on the man's side between the agent's Kevlar, which only protected his front and back.

The agent was a skilled fighter, though, and must have seen the punch coming. He dropped his elbow to intercept Green's punch, then turned it around to aim for his face. For one crazy moment, it looked to Green like the agent's arm was the crankshaft of an old steam-driven train, pointed almost directly at him.

The fist landed with enormous force, sending Green off balance and backward. He stumbled, struggling to get his feet back under himself, but momentum had shifted in favor of the agent. Another fist swung, this time an uppercut, catching Green's jaw, sending him farther away. He blinked, refocusing his eyes, in enough time to see his opponent stepping up toward him to finish the job. That step was all the time Green needed.

Green stepped back with his right foot, then brought it forward and up, between the man's legs as he stepped toward him. Apparently, Kevlar may be standard issue, but a cup wasn't. The agent doubled over and gasped at the pain, eyes wide. Green saw his opportunity and charged, head-butting the man and slamming him up against the car.

He could have stopped there, but he wasn't Black. His quest did not include captives nor did his nature sway toward mercy. If he got into a real fight, it was to the death. Green pulled his knife out in a reverse grip and dragged it across the agent's throat, habitually stepping to the side to make sure he would dodge the blood spray that always followed that kind of swipe.

"Mercer?" the agent's shoulder walkie hissed to life as the man's body fell to the ground. "What's your status?"

Green froze. Should he answer? The only idea that came to mind was yes. "He's dead, alright," Green said, speaking gruffly into the man's shoulder while depressing the button. "It's kind of a mess, though, and in the road."

"Clean it up, then!" came the response.

Having spent much of his time in the Army coordinating specialized operations, working and communicating as a group had become second nature. "Roger that." Green let go of the walkie and the body shifted, settling under its own weight. What should he do? He had bought time, but how much? If he left now, they would know that the organization had found them and would relocate before they could move in on them and get Black out.

In staring at the body, such a similar size to his own, Green got an insane idea. They didn't tell the difference between their voices, right? Green could be Mercer. Of course, if this didn't work, it could get him killed. But leaving Black here to die alone wasn't an option. As quickly as he could, Green stripped the man of his equipment and donned it himself, stuffing the corpse into the trunk of the car. It was do or die now.

It didn't take me long to realize I was not good at keeping secrets from these people. As I interviewed, they all inevitably asked me why I was interviewing them. I tried to dodge the questions at first, but Scarlett immediately noticed how terrible I am at lying and called me out on it. Most people, on finding out, were both appalled and eager to help me, but I was not particularly desirous of starting a witch hunt. So I requested they keep the inquiry to themselves and go about their assigned tasks until I had narrowed it down further.

I looked down at my list. Black was crossed off as soon as I had written him down. Scarlett had alerted us to the possibility of a mole in the first place. Lavendar's phone records and rather excellent lunch proved that he had been occupied ever since the meeting. Silver's interview had taken a little finesse on my part, with traffic constantly going in and out, but in the end he was cleared too. Limey and Red had corroborated each other's stories. That left Cyan, Orange, Green, Gold, and Blue.

Blue and Gold were both at their jobs and would likely have to wait. Green had gone to follow up on a lead, according to Scarlett.

That left Orange and Cyan. I had intended to get to Cyan first, but it felt like he was avoiding me. Could that mean he knew already I was looking for a mole, and he was it? Impossible. Until now, Cyan had been by my side every step of the way. He had had ample opportunity to kill me, but hadn't taken it. Still, interviewing everybody was the only way to clear them.

"Cyan!" I shouted, hailing him as I spotted him in the hall.

"Yes?" he asked, impatient.

"Do you have a moment to talk?"

"I'm talking now, aren't I?" he responded, sour. What had gotten into him?

"In private," I corrected, trying to be nice.

Cyan gave me a look that read entirely as suspicion, but nodded and ducked into the closest room. I followed immediately behind him, closing the door as I did so.

It was the room I had first found myself in after being targeted by Markham, though the card table was empty this time, without Black typing away at a laptop. Cyan walked to the other side of the table and turned to look at me, waiting, but not bothering to sit. Where to start?

"What is it?" he asked after a momentary staring contest.

"Can you account for your whereabouts since this morning's meeting?" I asked, trying not to sound accusing.

"I've spent most of it with Saturday, some with you, and the rest of it with Orange, cleaning up your apartment. Is that a problem?"

"No," I responded. How could I calm him? "No problem. Have you made or received any phone calls during that time?" I hated doing this to him, but I had to be thorough.

Cyan pulled his phone out of his pocket and skidded it across the card table toward me. "Am I suspect of something? Is that why Saturday won't talk to me?"

I picked up the phone before answering him, but, as I had guessed, all of Cyan's calls and texts were accounted for. "Everyone is a suspect," I confessed. "I'm trying to figure out who is revealing our secrets to the government." I held the phone out to him, hoping to offer it back as a sign of good faith. He didn't take it.

Cyan's posture shifted as he comprehended what I was saying. However, he did not become any less hostile. "A mole? How do we know it's not you who's the mole? We've welcomed you into our ranks without a second thought. I wouldn't be surprised if —"

"I'm the target," I interrupted before Cyan could go farther down that rabbit hole. I, of course, knew I couldn't possibly be the mole, even if I wanted to. Lying went against my core values, as well as my skill set. Cyan's protests and phone log assured me of his sincerity, too. "Do you have any ideas who the mole could be?" I asked. He knew these people far better than I did.

In talking to everybody, I had, despite my best efforts, started to suspect Green. "Green?" Cyan answered after a moment. "He's had the most opportunity to converse with the other side. He's even our expert when it comes to them and their movements."

I heaved a shuddering sigh. I really didn't want for it to be anybody, but Green?

For the first time since before my meeting with Saturday, Cyan looked at me with sympathy. "Oh, no. I'm sorry."

"We haven't talked to him yet," I said. "Whoever it is won't get away with it, I promise. I can tell when someone is lying." The promise was as much to myself as it was to Cyan.

The man across from me softened even more and smiled at me. "You are the perfect person for this task. I have confidence in you."

"Thanks," I responded. I straightened my back and put on a brave face. If it was Green, then we could get this done sooner than if it was anyone else. "Do you know where Green is?" I asked.

Cyan took his phone from my hand and dialed. We stared at each other as it rang. I was really glad I wasn't Cyan just then, having to talk to Green. If it were me, I would likely give away the truth and give Green the chance to run, assuming he was guilty. On the fourth ring, it beeped, sending Cyan to voicemail.

"Hey Green, it's Cyan. We're having a little trouble with something. Call me back ASAP." Cyan touched the smartphone and put it into his pocket again. "Who's next on the list?" he asked me.

"Orange," I responded, looking down.

"I think I know where he is."

"Cyan?" I said, catching him before he left. "Don't tell anyone yet?"

"Of course not." The old, comfortable Cyan was back, and I was pleased to have him on my side.

11

The child's cereal set heavily in Black's stomach. Not only was it entirely junk calories, but the small meal did little more than remind his body of just how empty it was. The milk revived him somewhat, but even that felt like it was too little too late.

The soreness in his shoulder ebbed, though, after about half an hour. Black's first thought was that the food had restored him some, but the timing was oddly suspicious. His rebelling stomach and Mother's penchant for chemicals and drugs led him to the conclusion that she had laced his meal with something.

Once he had realized that, a part of Black panicked. She was winning! He wished it wasn't true, even welcomed the soreness and pain over her control, but it was gone. Black rolled his shoulder and twisted his arm, searching desperately for the injury to make him even wince. No matter what he did, though, the pain was gone.

What now? The buzzing still edged at his mind. Think! He hit his forehead with the flat of his hand, as if that would catalyze his thoughts again. He could sleep. Maybe more than an hour, since he couldn't feel the shoulder to stop him. Then, at least, he wouldn't be conscious until the drug wore off, and he'd be able to rest his body and catch up on the much-needed slumber.

Black settled on the cold floor to sleep, using his arm as a pillow, but couldn't get his eyes to stay closed. He needed to rest! But what if Mother walked in as he slept? The things she could do to him then made him shudder. How much more miserable could she make him? Considerably, Black imagined.

But he needed to fight her, and to do that, he needed to keep – and recover, if he was honest with himself – his senses.

Despite the cold, Black slowed his breathing, consciously slowing his heart rate with it. He tried to think of nothing, just resting his eyelids without squeezing and searching for the sound of his heartbeat underneath the buzz. Calm. Finally, that sweet stillness enveloped him and rest came.

Green was used to doing security work. The routine of walking in circles for hours had no real effect on him. The undercover work, though, that was more Cyan's territory than his. It took every bit of knowledge he had collected on the enemy to maintain his lies. Unfortunately, he couldn't just punch everyone who suspected him.

So he kept his head low and followed along. At that particular moment, Green's duties put him inside the compound.

"Mercer!" someone yelled. That was for him. Green turned around as the man jogged up to him.

"Yes?" Green asked, adopting the coarse voice of the man he had killed as best he could. His pocket started buzzing again with his personal phone. Swiftly, Green touched the button on top through the fabric of his pants, making it stop again.

"A bunch of us are going to the pool hall tonight. You're welcome to join us, you know."

Green nodded curtly, but inside he was glowing. It was a way out and a way to get any information he gathered here back to the organization. "I'll think about it," Green said, making an effort to keep his voice gruff. "I could really use a drink."

"And some local tail, am I right?" The man slapped Green's shoulder. "There is this one chick that's almost always there. Smoking hot, drives a sweet car. I think I'm gonna land her tonight." Scarlett. Green knew that scene and she was the only one who fit that description.

"I bet you a hundred bucks I'll get her tonight, not you," Green said. Not that he would be sticking around to collect, if all went well.

The man patted Green's shoulder twice and pointed at him as he walked away. "Don't forget. Big day tomorrow – you've gotta be here. 8 o'clock, sharp. Can't have too much fun!"

Green laughed, hoping he looked less awkward than he felt. What should he do next? Green snapped as he pointed back at the man. They parted ways and Green heaved a sigh of relief as he continued down the hall, aimless beyond exploration but doing his best to appear purposeful. He had gotten to know the outside relatively well, but the inside was where the valuable information was.

The top story was pretty straightforward. It was in a U shape, with the open part being where they received any incoming traffic and supplies. Inside, there were rooms full of crates and ammo, a couple of surprisingly normal-looking business offices, a break room for patrolmen and the like, and an elevator.

That was what he needed to look into.

Green heard footsteps approaching from around the corner, ahead of him. Unsure what to do, Green ducked through the closest door, into one of the offices. He hopped onto the computer there, thinking that it would appear more explainable, if nothing else, assuming whoever it was caught him there instead of crouching in the corner of the office.

More to look like he was busy than to actually find any information, Green moved the mouse and opened the most recent program, the email server. There was another program, too, one he didn't recognize, but clicked.

A username and password box popped up. Great. He didn't have any ability in the digital world. Half the time, even when he did know his username and password, he still managed to mess it up.

Limey was really the one who was good at this, not Green. Their code names may have something in common, but that and the organization was where the similarities ended. What would Limey do here?

Green glanced around the desk again. Very little in the way of personal items. Green didn't even know whose desk he occupied. But then he found what he sought, taped to the side of the monitor. A slip of paper, maybe two inches squared. Typed clearly on it was a username and password. Could it really be that easy?

Green typed it in with his pointer finger, taking his time in an effort to be precise. After he hit enter, he looked at the screen again. The little wheel spun for a moment, then blinked, opening the program to the latest project. He had no idea what he was staring at, but knew that those at the organization could likely understand it.

Limey would know. Green pulled out his phone – four missed calls and one voicemail – and opened the camera feature. Slowly and steadily he worked his way through the documents and pictures, snapping his phone at each.

Green felt pretty proud of himself when he had enough and stopped. He could go on for hours with all he could get from this computer, but had to stop now. There was no way he could send all of them without raising a flag or some kind of alert to the government. A few though, could slip through the masses undetected. To ensure that the government didn't think to look past the first one, if they looked at all, Green took a selfie with as much of the office around him in the picture as he could get without raising suspicion. Then he picked a few pictures from his camera roll at random, hoping they meant something more to Limey than they did to him.

Just before hitting send, Green stopped. There was a mole in the organization. What if it was Limey? It could be anybody. Who could he trust? White. She would get the pictures to a trustworthy source. He backspaced Limey's name out of the address bar and put White's in, then hit send.

Cyan's phone buzzed at the same time as White's. Simultaneously, they pulled their phones out and looked. Breanne was calling him. What did his sister want? She should be in school right now.

"It's from Green!" White said excitedly. Cyan immediately put his phone down in favor of looking at White's. Whatever it was his sister wanted could wait.

Scarlett was back in the room, too, and she hurried over. Cyan had gone through the rest of the list with White. Orange was first, then they managed to catch Gold and Blue on their lunch breaks. Green was the only name on the list that was not crossed out, but Scarlett stood by him adamantly.

"Can we trust him?" Cyan asked as she opened the file.

White scoffed at the first image. It was a picture taken by and of himself, in uniform in an office Cyan didn't recognize. "What was he thinking?" White asked to no one in particular.

"He's worried about being watched," Scarlett interpreted. "He must have found his way into the enemy stronghold." Cyan knew from a previous discussion that Scarlett believed Green to be innocent. Cyan, however, was not so convinced. Yet.

White swiped the screen, exposing the next picture. It was taken of a computer screen, out of focus. "Can you clarify that?" Cyan asked her. She had already proven herself adept at cleaning up and refining camera imagery.

White smiled, glancing up at him. "If you find a way to sharpen an out-of-focus shot, Cyan, you'll be a millionaire." Cyan didn't bother to point out that he was already a millionaire; he understood what she meant.

Another swipe of the smartphone revealed another picture taken of a computer screen. "These must have been taken in secret," White said. "That's the only way not to have left a trace that he sent them to us."

"Scarlett, can you take the phone to Limey?" Cyan asked. He needed to discuss what this meant on the mole situation with White. Scarlett's opinion was already clear.

"Sure." Scarlett took the phone out of White's waiting hand and glided out of the room. Opposed as their opinions happened to be at that moment, she was still incredibly attractive.

"Why on earth would he send those to us if he were the mole?" White asked, bringing Cyan's attention back to the task at hand.

Cyan waited for Scarlett to be out of earshot before answering. "I was wondering the same thing." He looked at White again, whose face always radiated sincerity and, at that particular moment, genuine concern. "Maybe he's looking to be a triple agent? Those pictures were hard to read." Cyan doubted the Army grunt had that kind of acting skill, but if he was the mole, he must have.

"That's from a lack of skill, though. Camera phones have trouble focusing on objects too close to it. That error was probably ineptitude, not desire to get it wrong." The reporter knew her cameras, at least.

Cyan was forced to conclude, as Scarlett had been trying to tell him, that Green was innocent. He had put himself directly in harm's way so that they could have a man on the inside there. That was exactly Green's kind of logic, too. They had a mole in their ranks? Now the organization had one in the government's.

"If not Green, then who?" Cyan asked her.

"I don't know." White looked away. Was that shame?

"Hey," Cyan said, touching her on the shoulder to comfort her. "This is not your fault. We'll find him."

"Saturday trusted me to find the mole. I've tried, but I've run out of places to look. Worse, the mole must know by now that we're looking for them and think he's gotten away with it." She refused to make eye contact with him.

"That gives us the upper hand, then." Cyan tried to be comforting, but unfortunately she was right. "Let me see your list again."

She handed it to him, clearly resigned. Cyan looked over the list, filtering out the names he had been there to interview. Perhaps her straightforward and trusting nature had deceived her when she didn't have him to back her up.

Scanning the list, one thing stood out. Silver. The name had only one line through it. Had she interviewed them both at the same time?

"Did you talk to both Silvers?" he asked. It was before he himself had been vetted.

"I did talk to Silver. What do you mean, both?"

That was it! Cyan smiled in spite of himself. He forced himself to regroup before speaking. "Silver is a twin. Both twins, to be exact. They, together, make sure they know where anyone in the organization is at any point in time." Cyan could see the revelation dawning on her.

"It's a perfect place to be, too. They know it all without being in any real danger. How could I miss it?"

"How could you know?" He stopped, glad to see the light and fervor return to her eyes. "Which one did you talk to, do you remember?"

"The older one?" she responded, giving him an intentionally blank look. "They're twins. How do I tell them apart?"

"One has a cane," Cyan informed her. That was how he told them apart, at least.

"Ah." She searched her memory briefly. "This morning's interview did have a cane, yes."

Cyan smiled. "You go on – I'll follow in a minute." He couldn't neglect his sister for too long, even if she was just trying to get him to help her ditch school again.

He grinned at the thought, touching the button on this phone to listen to the voicemail.

"Please, I'm sorry I ditched. I won't again, I promise. Please, just get me out." Concern rippled through him. What on earth would entice her to leave this kind of voicemail? Was it a joke? One in poor taste, to be sure. "Please," she kept begging.

"What?" A new voice, coarse and deep and clearly masculine, sounded in the distance.

"Please!" Breanne's voice changed direction, away from the microphone on her cell. "Don't hurt me. I didn't do anything wrong. Ple–" Her pleas were cut short at the same time glass shattered on the line, no more than maybe ten feet from the receiver. Then nothing but sounds of muffled cloth, followed by steps, gradually growing louder. Someone clearly picked up the phone, grunted once, then a click.

Cyan couldn't even take the phone down from his ear. The horror of what he had just heard filled him.

They had his sister.

He stared ahead, wide-eyed, making efforts just to blink. Only the gentle voice of his phone interrupted his thoughts. Could it have even been real? Maybe he had imagined the whole thing? He prayed beyond all hope that he had.

"Are you still there?" the singsong voice on the phone asked. Cyan slowly pulled it down and stared at it before hitting the button to make the voicemail to play again. He needed to hear it again. Just to be sure.

When I approached the elevator, Silver smiled at me.

"Back again, miss?" I glanced down – the man was leaning on a cane. The same one I had spoken to earlier this morning. "Is there anything I can do for you?"

"Yes, actually," I responded. How did I approach this? Every scenario in my mind seemed indelicate, in the least. I forced myself to move forward. This was to get to the truth, at whatever cost of awkwardness it would be to me. "Have you seen your brother since we last spoke?"

Silver did a good job of hiding it, but I did detect some surprise in his demeanor.

"Cyan told me you have a twin," I explained. "Where might I find him?"

"Is this about what we spoke of this morning?" Silver asked delicately, always collected.

"I just want to cross his name off my list." I held my hands out, attempting to appear as unthreatening as possible. What I had said wasn't entirely a lie. I did want to clear him, but someone was guilty and at that moment, in my mind at least, he was the main suspect.

"Of course, miss. Of course." The man quieted and leaned on his cane.

I waited for a moment. Was he going to speak again? When it seemed the answer to that question was no, I spoke up. "Do you know where I might find him?"

In answer, the man pointed his cane to the lit indicator above the elevator doors. Then I understood. Part of Silver thought there was a chance his twin might be guilty, but didn't want to incriminate him out of loyalty. I might have done the same, were I in his position.

The elevator sounded and the light turned off. A moment later the doors opened and a carbon copy of Silver, minus the cane, walked out. "Hello, miss," the copy said, nodding to myself and his brother.

"May we speak for a moment?" I asked, indicating to the room I had just left.

Suddenly, Cyan rushed out of the door as I pointed toward it. Without a word to myself or either Silver, he jammed his hand into the closing elevator door. The doors opened again at his touch, and the lithe man slipped in and jammed the button that closed the door again, simultaneously pressing a button on his phone and bringing it to his ear again.

Odd, but okay. I could talk to Silver without him. I resolved to ask him about it when I had the chance, but had another task ahead of me at that moment.

Cyan had left the door open, but Silver let me through first. In my experience, both of the men I had called Silver had been nothing but gentlemanly to me.

"Close the door?" I asked as he followed me in.

"What can I do for you, miss?"

"Can I ask you a personal question?" I hoped to put him at ease. What would I do once I proved him guilty, if that were the case? I should have thought this whole thing through a little bit better.

"Go for it." The older man smiled gently. Doubts about this man's guilt spread through me. I could usually tell if someone was lying, but at that moment it would require me to ask the right questions.

"How did you come to join the organization?"

I watched Silver shift his weight, then head to the mini-fridge that held water bottles. "My brother got me into it. It was about three years ago. Why?" He got out two bottles and opened them both, handing one to me.

I took it and drank. Somehow it felt like the tables had shifted already, and he was the one asking all the questions. "I figured everybody's story couldn't have been as dramatic as my own," I answered.

"You'd be surprised," he said, drinking too.

"I have been. There is no normalcy here, is there?" I laughed, trying to feel comfortable with the man.

"Why don't you tell me what's really on your mind?" he asked, eyeing me with a stern paternal stare.

Then I got an idea. "I think your brother may be working for the government," I said, seemingly confessing but making an effort to keep an eye on Silver. If innocent, he should defend his brother, right? If guilty, I didn't know what he'd do.

Silver froze momentarily, then relaxed. "There's no mole." It was a pretty bold conclusion, but his tone had a calming effect over me. "Why would you think that?" He took a drink from his bottle and I did also, matching him and giving myself time to think. He hadn't defended his brother, but hadn't done anything dramatic that gave himself away, either. I decided the truth wasn't a good idea to answer his question in this case. I hated to lie, though, so I changed the subject.

"Have you ever seen your brother do anything suspicious? Something that took a lot of explaining?"

Silver's brow furrowed, and he looked up and to the right before speaking. "Now that you mention it, he did start using his phone to make calls to unknown numbers about four months ago." Liar! I knew it! It was a good lie, veiled in truth, though I could tell the difference. The story itself may be true, but likely of himself, not his brother.

I immediately wanted to call in help, but might be able to gain more insight if I played along just a little longer. He took a drink and I matched him again. Suddenly an oddly familiar wave of dizziness swept over me. Come on, the news wasn't that dramatic!

"What else have you noticed?" I asked, finding a seat and trying to contain myself and focus on his answer. It was like I was suddenly intoxicated.

"I once let somebody out I didn't recognize. I think my brother may have let him in. Does that help?" A blatant lie this time. Nothing to be gleaned there. I was grateful for the folding chair I had found, though.

What had he asked? Oh, yeah. "Yes, it does help. Do you remember when that was?"

"About six weeks ago." A hint of truth behind that lie. Huh? What had happened six weeks ago? I would have to ask Saturday when I got the chance.

I took another gulp of water, hoping the coolness would refresh my senses and snap them out of their odd stupor. It didn't help. If anything, I felt worse. I tried to speak – to ask another question – but the words garbled in my mouth. I could see and hear him just fine, but couldn't command anything in my body.

"Finally," the old man muttered, catching me as I started to fall forward. The man's entire demeanor shifted, like an actor exiting the stage and becoming himself again. It took me far too long to realize the water he had given me was laced with something.

The last thing I remember was the door opening from the outside as Silver was reaching for something in his pocket.

12

"I have another treat for you, Black."

Mother's voice sounded close to his ear, waking him. He had finally found sleep, and she had to wake him? Of course she did.

It took a moment for him to comprehend her statement. "I don't want another treat," he said, sitting up. The last treat had hurt his collarbone. It was throbbing again, and he knew her drugs were wearing off. He wasn't sure he could handle another fight.

"Of course you do," she said. She was kneeling beside him. How long had she been there, watching him sleep? Part of him knew he should be disturbed by the thought, but most of him didn't care anymore. "I bring you a different kind of pleasure this time." At that, she stood, revealing what looked like a pile of hair and clothes behind her. He rubbed his eyes, trying to clear them. The pile changed into a young girl, clearly unconscious, if not dead. Concern immediately filled him.

"What did you do to her? Is she okay?"

"She's alive, if that's what you're asking. I'm not a monster." Everything in his conscience begged to differ, but Black bit his tongue. "You're not gay, I assume?"

It was then Black understood Mother's intentions for the girl, and for him. "No. No way. I won't."

"Of course you will. Don't you think she's pretty?"

Hair covered the girl's face, but she couldn't have been older than high school. She clearly made efforts for her appearance, and he would likely have been attracted to her, were he in middle school again.

"She is pretty," Black admitted. "Still, not going to happen."

"It's your choice, of course," Mother said, striding for the door. For a moment, Black's hope soared. Could it be that she would really let this go? His hopes were dashed as she spoke again. "It's either you now, while she won't remember anything, or, if you wait until she wakes up, I'll give her to my men to do with as they please. Like I said, the choice is yours." With that, Mother smiled and closed the door behind her, leaving the young girl unconscious in the room with Black.

As soon as the door closed, Black crawled across the cold floor to the girl. Her pulse was faint but steady. Nothing he did roused her. There was no doubt – Mother was good at what she did.

The awful choice that lay before him renewed in his mind. Of course he couldn't do anything to her. At his peak, Black wasn't so sure he wouldn't have. He would have chosen what was best for the girl, regardless of personal sacrifice. Being the victim of only one man and not remembering was better for her than any of the horrors that would lay in her future if she were handed over to government grunts.

But now, Black just couldn't. He was becoming weaker; Mother was winning.

Maybe, if she woke, he could protect her? Black stared at the girl, past his weakened shoulder and arm, for who knows how long, going through every possible scenario in his head he could imagine. But, in every one, Mother won in the end. The only chance he saw for the girl was for Black to plead directly to their captor.

"Mother!" Black shouted, still waiting next to and watching the girl. "Mother!" She had heard him, he had no doubt, but how long would it take her to come back in? "Mother!"

Finally the blonde chemist reentered Black's cell. She glared at him from the doorway. "What is it?" she snapped. It was clear that he had done nothing with the girl, he knew. As he looked, the girl stirred for the first time. His shouts had probably disturbed her.

"Please," Black nearly choked, knowing he was begging. "Put her back. She has nothing to do with us. I'll do anything you ask. Anything at all. Just please, don't do this. Don't ruin this girl's life."

Mother raised an eyebrow. "You say you'll do anything, but you're already at my mercy. What more could you offer?"

Black had his answer ready. "Carte blanche. Anything you want, I won't fight you. Just don't make me do this. I've been resisting you; I won't anymore. That's what you want, isn't it?"

The girl stirred again. This time her eyes fluttered before closing again.

Mother contemplated Black's words. "What guarantee do I have that you'll obey next time?" she asked, coldly calculating the risks.

Emotion rose in Black's throat. "You have my word. That's all I have left, but I give it to you." What if she said no? What then? The girl was waking already. Mother would surely let her cronies loose on the girl.

Black stared at Mother for what seemed to be a lifetime, but in reality couldn't have been more than fifteen seconds. Then, finally, Mother nodded. She had agreed to his proposal! He wanted to spring up and hug her.

"Thank you!" Black gasped, louder than he intended to be.

The girl opened her eyes at his voice, waking fully.

As soon as she saw him, shirtless as he was, she recoiled, scooting back on her haunches before standing. "What did you do to me?" she asked accusingly as she stood. She touched under her hair– that was probably how they had drugged her, like they had the reporter: a needle to the neck.

"You sick freak!" Honestly, he didn't care what she thought of him, so long as she would be safe.

"Come here, dear," Mother said warmly. The girl turned and fled to her. The sight made Black sick to his stomach, but he was helpless against it.

Green heard the commotion in the break room and came over to investigate. Angry shouts echoed through the hall as he walked Mercer's assigned route. He glanced in just in time to see a punch thrown at the man that had invited him to the pool hall earlier. What was his name again? Fischer. The man dodged to one side and threw a fist at his opponent under the chin. That was all it took – the man who threw the first punch teetered slightly before falling backward.

Fischer bobbed his fists like a boxer. "Anyone else? Eh? She's mine first."

She? Green decided it was time to step in. The moment he did, he heard a sobbing from the corner under the ruckus the men were causing. Breanne? What on earth was she doing there?

"She's mine," Green said impulsively.

"Come on, Mercer, you can't get all the tail around here." Fischer kept his hands up. It only took Green a moment to size up the man. He had no gear on beyond the standard utility belt. A tight-fitting black shirt made no effort to hide his muscles. Clean-shaven and short cropped hair – nothing to hold on to. That was fine. He kept his kneecaps in the same place as anybody.

"You can have the babe at the bar," Green said, knowing it wouldn't take much to get Scarlett to agree. "I'll even help you land her. This one's mine, though."

"Oh yeah? Come and get her, then." Fischer bounced on his feet. Clearly the best way to protect Breanne was to establish dominance with these men. Green took off his Kevlar and set his guns on the table. Dominance meant fighting on even turf. Otherwise he would never earn their respect and ruin any future chances to. Though he was not generally inclined to intentionally weaken himself before a fight, he did so this time.

The rest of the men grew silent with anticipation, forming a circle around Fischer and Green. Green intentionally circled right, so that if Fischer were to strike, it was likely to be with his left, which was statistically the weaker hand. Fischer countered Green's movement, practically dancing as he moved. Green kept his eyes on Fischer, but was keenly aware of everyone in the room.

He let the rotating go on until his back was to Breanne. This both put himself between her and her primary threat in the room and made it so she would have a harder time recognizing him. He had regularly worked as a bodyguard at her home, and the girl could easily blow his cover once she realized Green was the same guy. He had to wait until they were alone before that happened.

Once he stood between them, Green stopped, and Fischer took that as an opportune time to strike. He jabbed quickly at Green – right, right, left – all of which he diverted, pushing the fists easily aside and past Green's core. Not to be outdone, Fischer followed it up by swinging his right fist out and around in a wide haymaker. Clearly the man was a boxer.

Green, on the other hand, watched a lot of pro-wrestling growing up. He stepped in and under the approaching fist, and stretched his right arm out, using Fischer's momentum against his own arm to clothesline the man.

Fischer fell spectacularly onto his back with an audible thud. The room was silent as they watched him struggle to catch his breath again. Green wasn't sure that would be enough to establish himself over these people, though. Their eyes were still on Fischer. So he spun around, kicking the man in the thigh with the standard-issue steel toe boots. Any harder and Green could have dealt permanent damage, but he decided not to this time. Fischer went from laid out flat to curled up, clutching his upper leg and yelping like a wounded dog.

Green didn't need to take his time kneeling in order to be intimidating, but did so in this case. The small bones in the palm beneath the pinkie were among the most common injuries for boxers. Green took the man's right hand in his own, peeling it off the leg. The yelp turned to a scream, broken off by gasps of pain as he torqued the hand. Green knew without looking that he had their audience's full attention now.

Green leaned in to Fischer's ear, though he spoke loudly enough to be heard by all. "The girl is mine," he grunted. Then he threw the hand to the ground and stood again. Heads raised, following him up. It felt good to command this kind of respect, he had to admit. When in the Army, he had earned the respect of his comrades through his leadership. He had never taken it before, not like this. Green strode over to Breanne, who was huddled in the fetal position, face and hair wet from tears.

It took almost no effort to pick her up and fling her over his shoulder. She couldn't have weighed more than a hundred pounds. With his free hand, he picked his gear up off the table. The group of onlookers moved out of his way wherever he stepped, but did not break their stares.

An empty room was easy to find down the hall from where the whole thing had taken place. Green dumped Breanne in the far corner of it before going back to close the door behind him.

It was once the door closed that Breanne screamed. Really? Now?

Green turned around and looked at her. "Breanne, stop." Upon hearing her name, silence consumed the room again. Green came and knelt by her, looking her in the eye and letting her recognize him. Fear drained from her face, replaced by relief, but it would probably take years before the horror of what had nearly happened to her would fade to the background. He would be surprised if it ever faded from her memory entirely.

She sprang from her corner and hugged him, arms wrapped tightly around his neck. "Thank you," she sobbed in his ear.

"It's okay," he said, gently rubbing her back. "You're safe now. I won't let them touch you."

The girl's sobs renewed with fresh vigor.

Green sat there with her for at least ten minutes, trying to be consoling, but really feeling much less comfortable than he had when fighting Fischer.

Finally the tears eased, and Green seized his chance and pulled away. "Breanne, can you do something for me?"

The girl nodded, wiping away her tears. She may as well be shoveling a driveway in a snowstorm. "Anything."

Where was his gear? By the door. Green stood and went to it, pulling his phone out. "This has some very important information on it. I need you to get it to your brother. Can you do that for me?"

"Yes, I can do that." The look she gave him told Green that she didn't really have a clue to the expanse of the situation, but she would follow his orders.

"Good. Tell him I will contact him via your phone when I get the chance."

"I don't have my phone anymore," she said, head down. "They took it."

"That's okay. I can get it." Green hoped to convey to the girl that he had a plan that stretched beyond what he had told her, but he was really just making it up as he went along. He needed Cyan to come up with the plan. Green was better at executing plans given to him when it came to this sort of subterfuge stuff.

"Not right now, Green," Cyan said immediately after answering the phone call.

It had been two and a half hours since he had gotten the voicemail from Breanne. Cyan had gone to the school, where he learned his sister had ditched, then to the mall, where there was no sign of her friend's car in the parking lot.

To home next. There he found a book on the back patio and the glass table shattered. That was where Cyan assumed she had called him from. No blood to speak of, but that proved hopeful in his mind that he would find his sister intact.

Next he would head to the security booth at the front gate. That building held access to any footage the cameras scattered about the property may have captured. Hopefully that would hold a video clue to the attackers. As of yet there was no ransom call, though. He didn't want to think what that meant.

A small, timid voice cut through the static and background noise of the phone's poor connection, pulling him out of his thoughts. "It's me." The owner of the voice was clearly not Green as Cyan's phone had indicated. Instead, the voice was female and clearly shaken.

Cyan stepped to where the reception was better. "Breanne? Is that you?" Hope soared. He stopped walking, focusing entirely on his phone now. Was this the ransom call?

"Yes."

"Are you alright? Have they hurt you? How many of them are there?"

"I'm alone." She broke into a sob. If they had abused her in any way, there would be no end to his wrath on them.

"Good. Explain to me where you are. I'll come get you. Are you inside?"

"I'm in a car. That security man told me to call you and wait here." Green. He must have been there to help. Cyan didn't know how to thank him. Later.

"Good." Cyan tried to keep his voice level as to not further stress his sister. "Lie down across the back seat. Can you do that for me?"

"I already am. He said —" Breanne's voice broke, but Cyan understood.

"Good, good. Can you explain to me what you see out the window without sitting up all the way?" Cyan started heading to his car. He had a good idea of where she might be. Green was undercover within the government. If Breanne had seen Green, it was a good bet they were both about ten miles east of town. From where Cyan currently stood, that would be about a twelve minute drive, if he sped. And he had all intentions of doing so.

"There's a lot of trees on this side of the road. Over there is some sort of office. It's the main crossroads from the freeway." That was all he needed. He knew the intersection. He dropped into one of the faster cars – the Bugatti – and the phone automatically connected to the Bluetooth, playing his sister's voice over the speakers of the car.

"Okay," he said, starting the car. "I'm on my way."

"Don't hang up." Breanne's request was quick and panicked. "Please."

"I won't. I'm right here. Just put your head down on the seat. I'll be there soon. "

For the entirety of the trip, Cyan did the talking. He could still hear her sniff, as if crying, and occasionally make other small sounds. She was there and listening, but Cyan knew just talking was the most comforting thing he could do for her until he picked her up. Even so, it felt like the longest ten minutes of his life.

He got to the intersection he had picked up Scarlett the previous night and pulled over. It was a quiet road this time in the afternoon. Breanne finally spoke to him again.

"I see you." Her voice cracked again.

"Good. Stay down." Cyan scanned the area, looking for Green's car more than his sister, assuming that's where she was. Then he spotted it, about two blocks south of the intersection with the freeway that had taken him there.

He turned around and pulled up beside the car, opening the passenger door from his driver's seat so she might get in faster. The road beneath his car was stained with red, but to Cyan's relief, Breanne seemed to be unhurt, at least physically.

He didn't wait for her to put her seat belt on or even close the door before he sped away again. The vigor from stomping the gas did the job for him.

"Are you okay?" Cyan asked again, risking a glance away from the road to her. She was the most disheveled Cyan had ever seen her, in his recollection, but truly a sight for sore eyes. "Did they touch you?"

Breanne was quiet for a moment, and in that second Cyan feared the worst. Then she shook her head. "They tried. They wanted to. But that security guy you hired for my birthday party stopped them. Did you send him?"

"I would have, but he was busy, or so he told me." Cyan knew he was rambling. "Just a case of right time, right place, I guess." It wasn't entirely the truth, but Cyan didn't want to expose her to any more of the tiny war he and the organization waged.

Breanne froze for a moment, then leaned forward and threw up onto the floorboard of the Bugatti. Cyan was fine with it – he could clean it up later. He rubbed her back for a moment as another round came up.

When she was done, Cyan reached back and fetched a water bottle from the seat behind her, opening it and offering it to her.

The government had struck a nerve by abducting her. There was no end of the earth to which they could hide and escape from him now.

13

Scarlett walked in the halls, toward the room where she had last seen Cyan and White. As she passed the elevator, she noticed something odd. Where was Silver? Maybe Cyan would know. She continued, finding the door closed but no voices were inside. She tried the door – maybe they had left? – but it didn't give.

Now alarm bells were starting to go off in her head. No doors beyond the restrooms stayed locked, not here. "Cyan?" she shouted through the door. "White?" Scarlett tried the door again. The knob turned, but the door itself didn't budge. "Cyan?" Were they okay? Scarlett wasn't yet to the point of panicking, but was quickly approaching it.

Saturday appeared around the corner and saw her. Yes! "What's wrong, Scarlett?" he asked, sensing her concern.

"Silver's gone, Cyan and White should be in here, but they're not answering, and the door has been wedged shut from the inside and I can't get in." Scarlett said the words in a rush, not caring about her appearance at the moment.

Saturday's eyes opened wide. Good – it wasn't just her imagination blowing things out of proportion. She stepped out of the way as Saturday tried the knob, coming to the same conclusion she had already reached. Then he stepped back and away. What did he know? Before she could ask, he rammed his shoulder as low on the door as he could comfortably reach, and it gave way.

Inside, Silver and White were both strewn awkwardly in the small room. White had collapsed, halfway fallen from a folding chair. Silver had been slumped against the other side of the door, holding it closed. Any filter holding the panic back from Scarlett was now gone, and the feeling overwhelmed her. White seemed to be sleeping uncomfortably, but Silver's eyes were open wide in a chillingly still terror.

Saturday was the first to move in, rushing ahead of Scarlett to Silver. The movement startled Scarlett into following, going to White instead. Saturday had more experience when it came to medical emergencies than she did, but she knew the human body well enough to find a pulse and determine its health.

White's skin was cold and clammy, but her pulse was detectable and steady. "She's alive," Scarlett called to Saturday. Saturday came over to join her, and she moved so he could examine White. "What about Silver?" Scarlett asked when Saturday didn't say.

"He's gone. Heart attack." Saturday was strangely unmoved by the statement, instead focusing entirely on White. Scarlett, however, felt the full impact of the statement. Silver? Gone? Scarlett looked over at the man, and instantly regretted it. Saturday had closed the man's eyes, but the posture suggested the man did not go comfortably. His hands were up close to his chest, both frozen solid in claw shapes. The right hand clenched the left arm, and the left looked like it had just released part of his shirt.

In everything, Scarlett couldn't help but notice what was missing from the scene: Cyan. Was he the mole? When Scarlett had last left the room, Cyan was alone with White, and Silver was just outside. Had White figured it out, and Cyan tried to kill her? She had a spilled water bottle next to her, likely the source of her current condition, if past experience with this division of the government was any indication.

"Get Orange," Saturday said, struggling to get White sitting upright against the wall.

Scarlett could hardly think, but she could obey. Grateful to leave the room, she bolted over to where she had last seen him with Limey.

"Orange!" she called as she approached the room. The odd man reached the door at the same time Scarlett did.

"What's up?" he asked, disturbingly casual compared to Scarlett's current state of mind.

"Saturday needs you in the break room." She beckoned him and he followed her back. Saturday had thrown a blanket over Silver and was back with White again.

"Thank you, Scarlett." Saturday still took the time to thank her despite the situation. That was part of what made him a good leader, she realized. "Can you get everyone to evacuate the building, please?"

Scarlett immediately turned to obey, but a thought struck her. "Who do we know we can trust?" Scarlett asked, turning back.

"The villain has already struck and disappeared. Anyone left here we can assume we can trust. But our location has been compromised, that much is clear." That made sense. Scarlett nodded and went back again to Limey's workspace, getting ready to help where she could. Saturday was right – they needed to leave as soon as possible.

Natasha stood just inside the door of Black's cell. She had turned the lights off about ten minutes ago, and Black had again used the restroom, this time taking off his pants and doing the same to them as he had to his shirt. Now he was naked, save for his boxer shorts. Natasha didn't mind. There was a psychological shift that changed even the strongest of people into scared animals when they felt exposed.

Black was more vulnerable now than ever before, and had obeyed her every request since she had taken the girl back. How long it would last, she didn't know. She just hoped she had broken him by the time he figured out what she had really done with the girl.

Men were taking in a table and out the soiled pants. She would dine with Black tonight. She had ordered steak and lobster, with fixings, and it was being brought in now. The light from the hallway was the only source in the room, but Black didn't move.

When everything was ready, the lights came back on. She had chosen an evening dress, in stark contrast to her "date". Black cowered in the corner as the room lit up again.

"Humphrey," she called to him. "Look at me, Humphrey."

He looked, but otherwise didn't move. That was fine; he was obedient.

"Come here," she called, patting her leg.

The man hesitated only briefly, deciding to do as she wished. It was clear that he was still obeying of his own will, not following her blindly without question. It would take the latter for her to really be able to trust him outside the room. It was a step in the right direction, however.

Slowly he reached the table and stood beside the chair, waiting to be invited to join her. He glanced at the food, probably smelling the savory meal.

"Sit."

He sat.

Natasha put the pills in her hand next to his water before sitting down herself. He stared at the food without touching it. "Help yourself," she instructed, pulling some biscuits from the cloth in a basket. All the food was shared between them, showing him that she and her food could be trusted.

He first reached for the ice water, though it was cool in the room, and drained it entirely. All delicacy expected of this kind of meal was gone from Black.

After a good three minutes of eating together in silence, Natasha felt she had waited for him long enough.

"Say something, Humphrey." She had spoken it as a request, but she was sure they both knew it was an order.

He swallowed before speaking. So he did remember some of his manners. "Am I supposed to take those?" he asked, indicating to the pills she had placed next to his glass.

"I'd like you to, but it's up to you. They're to help with your shoulder." It was an honest statement, but he had no way of knowing that. He was smart – she wouldn't have favored him like this otherwise – so he probably didn't trust her. But that made the game all more interesting.

Black's movements stalled as he chewed and contemplated his choices. Then, slowly, he swallowed his food and took the pills in his hand. She made no move to interrupt him now, watching with measured fascination. Then, he put them back down, deciding against taking them. For now.

"What else would you like to know?" Natasha asked.

"Is this a date?" She could see his mind churning, trying to wrap itself around the entirety of the situation.

"In a way. We're getting to know each other a little more."

"Is the girl alright?"

Natasha knew the honest answer was no. She had given the child to her men to do with as they pleased, despite Natasha's promise to let the girl go.

Abducting the child served several purposes. First, she had learned the weaknesses of many people within the organization from her man on the inside. If there was a second in command within the organization, it was Cyan. Taking his sister would not only destroy him, but therefore dramatically cripple the organization entirely.

Black would have been the next threat posed, and her man on the inside couldn't find a weakness or pressure point for him. So, Black was the one chosen to be sitting across from her now. If they still planned a rescue attempt for tomorrow, they'd have to do it without two of their most useful and most powerful members.

Natasha had decided on a whim to use the girl to manipulate Black, and, though unsuccessful in her original plan, the *carte blanche* was a welcome tool. The connection between Black and Natasha's other prisoner was just a pleasant stroke of luck.

"The girl is fine," Natasha lied, answering Black's question. "Why do you care?" She was genuinely interested in how he would answer.

Black took a bite before doing so, though. Color was returning to his face, making him appear healthier than he had all day. The food was strengthening him. Natasha made a mental note of it. "Degrading my existence is one thing," Black finally answered, also more collected than she had seen him lately. "But doing to the girl what you're doing to me would ruin her life. Especially after what you threatened." Black spoke almost casually, and with more words than she remembered him using since he arrived.

"That didn't answer my question."

A pause. "I deserve it. She doesn't."

Deserve it. Natasha savored the words. He was breaking. "You and she are not my only prisoners here, you know," Natasha said, sipping the wine she had poured. She was enjoying herself immensely, and was curious how Black would react to the information that his brother was nearby.

Her words didn't seem to faze him as he reached for the asparagus spears. "Who is it? Anyone interesting?" he asked, again too casual. It seemed he was putting on a laid-back character. Acting? Not really a style that suited him. But, then again, she had yet to break him fully. That would be an interesting moment, when that victory finally came.

"I think you know him as Monday," Natasha responded, watching him all the while.

Black froze for half a second as he processed the familiarity of the name and all it meant. Then he finished drinking his water and put it down. Definitely forced. Fascinating. "Monday is dead. Nice try, though." He may be acting casual, but now he was watching her, challenging her to prove him wrong. Did she detect a touch of hope in his glance, too?

"He isn't," Natasha played along. "How else would I know that he's your brother?" She had him there, and they both knew it. She sure enjoyed these games with him.

"Anna could have found that out," Black defended.

Natasha didn't need to argue to know that she had won. "Take your pills," she suggested.

Black picked them up again, contemplated them only a moment, and took them without asking about what they were and why. He would never be a pawn in her game, but he may end up her knight yet.

I woke up to Saturday carrying me. I was incredibly woozy, almost drunk, and would not likely have been able to walk, had I even had the thought. I must have made some sort of noise, though, because he spoke to me. His voice overlapped itself and sounded distant and echoey, yet loud enough to be heard.

"Hang on, White. Close your eyes. We're almost there."

It didn't occur to me to do anything else. So I waited, eyes closed, leaning close to the fatherly gentleman and seeking comfort in his stability. When he set me down – it could have been seconds or hours later and I wouldn't have known the difference – I dropped into a couch. My stomach churned with every movement and I savored being stationary again.

Saturday left my side and disappeared into the distance. I had trouble keeping track of mostly everything that

I wasn't in physical contact with. I rolled over on the couch, focusing all my efforts on just keeping my stomach contents in check.

"Don't fight it," Saturday said, suddenly reappearing with a small office trash can. "Better to purge your system of the poison now, before your body processes any more of it."

I didn't really comprehend most of what he said beyond the first sentence. Fighting it didn't feel like the most comfortable choice, anyway. So I threw up, making most of it into the trash can.

Saturday took his hand off my back to wipe his own face. "Keep going," he coaxed. "The more, the better."

I needed no more encouragement than that. On and on I went. I had no idea my stomach could hold that much. Finally I finished and Saturday removed the trash can and its sour contents. Exhaustion overwhelmed me then, and I fell back to sleep.

Cyan left his sister back at the estate with specific instructions to the staff not to let her leave. Not that Breanne had any inclination to. More than anything she wanted to be alone, and Cyan could respect that. He also knew she would turn to her diary and write, sometimes for hours, in times of stress. Today would definitely qualify.

Leaving her alone also allowed Cyan to go back and regroup with everybody. So he left, heading back to the office building in hopes of discovering something about Silver and the mole. White surely had to have an update by now.

There were no cars in the parking lot when he got there. That was odd. Maybe they had to hide them for some reason? He entered anyway through the empty bottom floor to the elevator. Pressing the button didn't do anything; no noise or light registered. What had happened? Did they evacuate?

Ah. They must have figured out who the mole was. Why not include him, though? White had cleared his name much earlier in the day.

He stepped back from the elevator as he pulled out his phone and called Saturday. The phone rang twice before the familiar voice picked up.

"Hello, Cyan."

"Hello. What happened? Did you guys evacuate?"

"We did. Where did you go? I couldn't find you in the building." Saturday's voice was very matter-of-fact.

"They took my sister. I couldn't wait. Silver and White all saw me leave. Where are you guys now?"

"Is Breanne okay?" Saturday asked. Cyan appreciated his concern, but couldn't help but notice he hadn't answered his question.

"She's alive and back home, but very shaken. Thanks for asking." Cyan paused, giving Saturday a chance to answer his previous question, but spoke again when Saturday didn't. "Where are you? I've a lot to discuss. Green managed to get me more information."

Silence reigned for a moment before Saturday's voice filled the line again. "I'm afraid I can't tell you that right now."

"What?" Cyan asked, not particularly caring about how polite he was at that moment. "Why not?"

"Are you aware we have a mole in the organization?"

"Yes, I helped White with the investigation. Just ask her – she'll tell you."

"White's out of commission for a while. Silver's dead, at least one of them. Scarlett told me she last saw them with you, and you disappeared about the same time. Tell me you understand how it looks to me."

Cyan understood exactly how it looked. He also knew, with this new information, the other Silver had to be the culprit as he had suspected hours ago. Unfortunately,

Cyan now seemed to be the only one who knew this, and he was the lead suspect instead.

"I get it," Cyan said after a moment, walking back to the car. "All I can say right now is that Silver is the mole, not me. I get not trusting me, but please, if my time in the organization," and their friendship, "means anything to you, please don't trust him either. At least until White recovers. Once you hear what she has to say, if she accuses me, then fine."

"You've that much faith she'll protect you?"

"We both know she'll be honest," Cyan said, smiling in spite of himself. "She and I know what happened. Unfortunately that means she is the only one that could clear me. If I may ask, do you have any idea how long that will be?"

Cyan knew Saturday was in no way obligated to answer him, but hoped to know at least how long he had to wait. He was sitting on information that could be best in Limey's hands, but they wouldn't trust it until he was cleared, even if it was originally from Green.

"Best guess," Saturday answered, "a couple of hours."

"Thank you." Cyan was genuinely thankful. "I will be at my home until you need me."

"Cyan," Saturday's voice echoed both emotion and strength. "Thank you for understanding."

"I want these guys gone as much as you do. If that means stepping aside until I can be helpful again, I get it."

"I'll let you know when I can," Saturday responded.

Cyan hung up the phone and sat in the car, unsure what to do or where to go now. All of his person wanted to pursue the people that had hurt his sister, but he knew it would be futile and maybe even counterproductive if he did so alone. His best chance was waiting until they could attack as one united force. Back home, then.

14

Green was on security duty outside again for the afternoon. It seemed that the routine would be to send one man out to investigate any disturbance, and if the results weren't favorable, the entire force would respond.

It was definitely good information to have, but usually meant a lot of fuss over nothing. Everyone in the group – including Green, in this case – was annoyed at the whole world whenever this happened. Cyan had even raised an alarm by stopping near the perimeter when he had come by, but had disappeared before the crew would have bombarded him in full force. It was enough to let Green know Breanne was safe, though.

Finally the time for his shift to end came. He went inside to put the gear back in Mercer's locker, being sure to keep the key card with him so he could get into the building later. He had felt very productive in learning more about their enemy and was eager to share what he had picked up with the organization.

"You're coming to the bar with us tonight, right Mercer?" Fischer's hand appeared on Green's shoulder from behind him, all animosity between them apparently gone. Green growled and looked at the hand, which was enough to make Fischer recoil.

"I'll be there." It was his best chance to contact Scarlett and the organization. The government insisted they all sleep at or near the compound in case of an emergency, but didn't mind them leaving on their off hours. Green planned to take as much advantage of this as he could.

"Good," Fischer started putting his gear away, too. "You owe me for earlier. You've gotta help me land that chick." *Owe* wasn't quite the word Green would have used, but he wouldn't argue the point.

"Did the higher-ups keep any of the girl's stuff?" Green asked, being sure to keep his voice as gruff as possible. He had yet to lay hands on Breanne's phone, which was to be his primary communication back to the organization.

"You want a trophy, huh? Can't say I blame you. Anything in particular?" Fischer pulled a box down from on top of the lockers.

"A girl like her? Her life is in her cell phone," Green grunted.

"I can do that." Fischer fished through the box. Why was he being so friendly? Green was suddenly rather suspicious. "Here it is!" Fischer pulled it out and handed it to him. Green took it and held it in his hand. Fischer smiled at him – a little broader than Green would have expected. What was his play?

"We're friends, right Mercer?" Fischer said, jovial.

Then he understood. Green had made a rather successful power play, and Fischer was trying to earn some respect back by being friends with him. Green owed Fischer nothing, and wanted nothing to do with these kinds of people. But he couldn't let that be known. What would Cyan do? Keep his options open, more than likely.

So Green responded to the man with what he hoped was a convincing smile, but made no promises or agreements.

Fischer beamed back, happily slapping Green's shoulder. "I'll see you there!" Fischer said, refreshing his deodorant and checking his teeth before departing.

As soon as the room was clear, Green opened the phone. He felt silly and absurd holding one covered in pink and rhinestones, but it served the purpose he needed it to. He booted it up without much difficulty and sent a period to

Cyan, letting him know that he had it in his possession without letting any information through, just in case the line was monitored.

Then he powered it down and slipped it into his pocket before heading out and catching a ride with Fischer to the pool hall.

Despite her personal desires, Scarlett went to the pool hall at Saturday's request. She wanted to stay at the safehouse until White regained consciousness, but Saturday was right – she was more useful where she could gather information. Saturday assured her that they were nearly done with that part and as soon as they interpreted whatever else Green had for them, they would solidify their plan to strike.

The one good thing about being sent this way was the possibility of talking to Green herself. All of this distrust was weighing on her. She liked being the deceiver, not the deceived. That may have been part of why Saturday had sent her here, now that she thought about it. He was like a father to them in a way – knowing what she needed before she herself did.

She had a couple of shots of Jack Daniels when she first arrived and invited herself to join the only players in the room at their table. They didn't seem to mind.

It didn't take much longer for the group of government men to storm in, laughing and joking with each other. As subtly as she could, Scarlett scanned each one for Green's familiar face. When she spotted him, she noted he looked extra grumpy. Scarlett made her shot, intentionally missing, and leaned her cue against the wall, wondering if she might get a word with him. Green could not only verify Cyan's story – or disprove it, if it came to that – but he could also give them information about what to expect for the assault tomorrow.

The man Green was speaking with broke off and angled for Scarlett before she could talk to her friend. "Hey, babe," the agent said, making it clear he would not leave her an escape route.

Scarlett smiled winningly at him and rocked her shoulders. "I don't think I've had nearly enough alcohol for this conversation," Scarlett responded, leaning forward.

Her words had the desired effect. The man jumped at the chance to buy her a drink, waving one hand at the bartender and leaving her alone to approach Green, who was sifting through the cues on the wall.

"I like the 21 ounce," she said in his ear.

Green spun quickly, fist in the air before realizing who was so close to him. He brought his hand down and sighed. A bit jumpy, wasn't he?

"What's wrong?"

"I'm not cut out for this undercover stuff," he said. She could feel the stress coming from him, though he did a good enough job at not projecting it to the rest of the crew. "This is Cyan's world, not mine. The things these people accept as normal..." Scarlett touched his shoulder, predicting he would shudder. It gave Green a bit of solace and gave anyone looking a reason for him to behave so out of character.

"You're doing well." She didn't know how else to comfort him. "This will all be over soon."

"How soon?"

Scarlett's paranoia from the day's hunt for the mole flashed in her brain, but she quickly shunned it. She could trust Green. She knew that much. And he depended on her, too. "Stay by your phone. We'll have a plan soon, I promise."

Green gave her an odd look. "Cyan has my phone. I gave it to his sister to give to him. Did she not?" Ah. Of his own accord, Green had verified Cyan's story. Scarlett couldn't let her friendship with Cyan get in the way, though. She needed to hear it from White before she was fully convinced.

"She gave it to Cyan, yes," Scarlett said, reserving the rest until he was in a less intense situation. She didn't need to add undue stress to the man. "We just need you right now to keep your head down and stay with these people. We'll let you in on the plan when we have one."

Green's expression changed as he noticed someone behind her. "And here's the guy I was telling you about," Green said, dropping his voice to a coarse grunt. He had spotted someone and was back to his cover character. He was better at this than he gave himself credit for.

Scarlett plastered a smile on her face and spun, facing the man she had brushed off earlier. He had returned, a pint in each hand. Clearly Green was trying to pair the two of them. Was the beer-wielder someone with power? Scarlett supposed it was about time she found out. She adopted her most seductive walk, accompanying the man to the table where he and his cohorts had set up to play.

Black felt revived after the first meal of real food in nearly two days. Not just revived. Empowered. Assuming that meal was actually at dinner time, it meant the day of his redemption was drawing closer. Maybe twelve hours left. He was feeling so good afterward he even treated himself to some exercises – something he hadn't done since he had first arrived in this hellhole.

Not only that, but he had learned something about Mother and her plans, too. This wasn't just about Black. This whole dance was about taking down the organization for good. She had told him from the beginning she planned on using him to move against them covertly. With the revelation of Monday being within reach, Black realized how close she was to that goal. With his past, which he still couldn't forgive himself for after six years, Mother probably assumed she could make history repeat itself. But Black would not turn his back on his brother nor the organization ever again.

Suddenly the buzzing dropped in volume. The sound had grated on him before, but now Black felt like nothing could stop him. The quiet was normally a harbinger of Mother, and Black looked to the door expectantly. After ten seconds or so, it didn't open. What was she up to this time? Black stood and stepped closer to the door, but no change. The lights turned off, but it was far too soon for another meal.

Then the screaming started.

It came over the speakers and flooded his cell. It was so loud Black could hear it echo from the walls of the small room. There was no tuning it out. The shouts of agony sounded familiar, much like his own scream when he had broken his femur in a hot zone overseas. The pain had seared through him, making him cry out with the same kind of vigor and sincerity that surrounded him now.

No, these screams weren't his, but they sounded like they could have been.

The screams were composed of pure pain. Muffled at first, as if through gritted teeth, then something happened that made the tortured man release a feral howl, open-mouthed and loud, until his lungs were empty. Desperate gasps followed, laced with whimpers. Four and a half breaths – was it over? – and the screaming renewed. Black didn't think it possible to be louder than it was before, but they managed it.

The cries shook him to his core. How one man could stand that much pain and not have passed out, Black didn't know. He himself had no memory of any events after about ten seconds following the building falling and snapping the bone in his upper leg. Now, Black found himself breathing heavily just to keep his own calm.

They were just sounds.

Sounds made by a man in unfathomable pain.

It clicked. Black understood why the cries sounded so familiar. He slammed face-first into the realization, like it was a brick wall and he a sports car. Mother had been telling the truth.

The screams didn't belong to himself, but to his brother.

The mere idea brought him to his knees as all strength left him. He clapped his hands over his ears, just wishing for it all to stop. His hands weren't even close to filtering or even muffling the sound of his brother's screams. Sympathetic tears came unbidden and Black made no effort to check them. Please, just stop!

The screams didn't, though. They eased slightly on occasion, but that only made the shouts of agony sound louder and fresher when they came again.

The torture continued for longer than Black thought possible. He was exhausted just by listening to it. They must have looped the sound at some point, but Black didn't care to listen closely enough to find out when. He was helpless in a black room, on his knees, covering his ears and weeping. Surely there was no greater torment than the one he was trapped in now.

15

I woke up with an involuntary groan and a pounding headache. It felt like the throbbing of a sore tooth but throughout my entire skull. I sat up and the sensation worsened. Lying down was more comfortable anyway. It was like the worst hangover ever. The light that filtered in the window was muted by either dusk or dawn. I had no idea how long I'd been asleep. I closed my eyes, savoring the darkness once again.

"White?" came a soft voice. The word still echoed in my skull, feeling like a shout. I opened my eyes again to see Saturday kneel next to me with a glass of water. "You're dehydrated. Drink up."

It wasn't until the coolness of the water hit my pallet that I realized the absolutely terrible flavor in my mouth. I sat up, slowly this time, to sip again, trying to rinse it out, and clasping the glass with both hands to ensure steadiness.

"What happened?" I asked when I finished the glass. Saturday took it from me and replaced it with fresh water in a mug bearing the symbol of a local real estate company.

"I was hoping you could tell me." Saturday's voice was a mix of concern and authority.

Recovering some, I glanced about the room. We were in a partially furnished – but appeared to be unlived-in – house. The place looked simultaneously cold and inviting. The couch I had woken up on was a tan color. It complimented the cream carpet, but there were no pictures on the walls or rings from condensation on the wooden table to show it had been used for drinks. No magazines nor books scattered about. Most obviously, the place was wholly new to me.

It took me a moment to comprehend Saturday's question and compile an answer. Every thought was slow and dragging. "I remember I was talking with Cyan..." I started. The name stirred a subtle shift in my one-man audience, but at the moment I had no capacity to contemplate why. "He told me there are two men named Silver? I was working on the list, to find the mole. I had cleared one Silver, but not the other. Cyan got a phone call and left, so I talked to the other Silver alone."

"Cyan left? What was on the call?"

"I don't know who called him. I just know that he was," I struggled to find the right word, "panicked when he left."

Saturday nodded, clearly understanding more than I did. "Continue," he requested. "What happened next?"

"I talked to Silver. The other Silver." My thoughts stopped in their tracks as I remembered, then comprehended what happened next. "Silver! He's the mole!" I stood, desperate to do something. To stop him. My head swam. Saturday stood too, putting his hand on my shoulder to coax me down. I complied, realizing there was nothing my eagerness could do to help at the moment. Saturday sat next to me on the couch.

"Go on," he said after a moment, patient but clear he needed to know more. I took a bracing gulp of the water and proceeded with my tale.

"He got a water bottle from the fridge. One for each of us. As we spoke, I just kept feeling worse. The last thing I remember was Silver reaching for his pocket and the door opening. Was that Cyan? What happened? Where is he?" I asked the last few questions quickly. I expected him to be there, after all the help he had offered me earlier.

"As best I can understand it, it was Silver – the good one – that came to your rescue. He defended you from his brother." Saturday stopped and swallowed, breathing deeply before continuing. "At the cost of his life, I'm afraid."

Saturday's words sank in like an anchor in my soul. Silver had died? Protecting me? I had only spoken to the man in passing over the last couple of days. The fact that he had fought his brother for me – a woman he barely knew – was unfathomable. My brain certainly took its time to comprehend the thought.

Saturday slapped his hands on his knees and stood, startling me out of my reverie. "We will mourn later. We cannot sit idly by while they still have one of our men. The time to strike back upon us." He offered his hand to me, like some hero from a silent film. "Can you stand?" he asked me.

"I think I can," I said, taking his hand and smiling in spite of myself.

It took Monday an hour to pass out from Natasha's work. She took her time, for sure. She had learned long ago that the art of physical torture, which was by no means her preference, was valued in duration rather than aggression.

A concoction of pills created the desired canvas for her. Over the course of a couple of hours, she used one tablet to shut down the man's pancreas, putting him into a lethargic stupor. One more simulated peripheral neuropathy, like one who had advanced diabetes. It made his nerves feel as if they were both asleep and on fire simultaneously. Every nerve would light up with sensitivity at the lightest touch. A breath on his skin felt like a burning shove; a prod became a stab.

Once her cocktail took effect, she ordered the microphones be opened for her audience. This was all about breaking Black, after all. She could have just threatened to kill Monday, but this way felt much more real. More... elegant.

It was amazing how the body functioned. Natasha marveled at the chemistry of a body, and loved to find its limits. She definitely preferred torturing men to women, at least when it came to physical pain. Women naturally had a higher pain tolerance, especially under stress. The trick was to not let her victim pass out or go into shock. It was a fine line, one that took practice to tread masterfully. She didn't mind practicing it now, either. Every time she did, she learned something new.

Monday was a special pleasure – one she had reserved for an occasion like this. She had gotten to know him over their years together. He had shared his opinions on most everything from opera to biker gangs at one time or another. He even knew a fair amount about her. They had a connection, in a special sort of way, and that made the experience all the more enjoyable. Unique.

Lewitt had once advised her to kill Monday and be done with him, but this experience? Natasha was pleased she hadn't.

Now she sat in her office, writing everything in her logs. She twiddled the pen in her hand, reminiscing with a smile. Not anytime soon, but she would like to try this little experiment again, if the occasion arose.

She had a more imminent threat at hand, though. Assuming the organization still planned on attacking tomorrow. Preparations had been made. The guard doubled, the organization's most powerful members crippled. The only thing left was to let the rest of them come to her. Then she could tame them, too.

As if the thought summoned him, the one they called Silver beeped at her door, their secure way of asking for permission to enter. She held down a doorbell-esque button under her desk until the older man pulled the door open and entered.

"Hello, Jack." Natasha capped her pen and put aside her log as he entered. He sat in the chair opposite her, waiting to be addressed further. She had to assume he had been exposed within the organization and couldn't help but wonder what he wanted now. "What can I do for you?"

"I want out," he spat without preamble. Natasha knew he was aware that wasn't his choice. She scowled at him, but he continued. "Look, my brother is dead. Anyone who thought they were my friend is wiser now. I serve no purpose to you now that I'm exposed. Please, just give me my money and let me walk away. I won't tell a soul." Natasha got the impression the speech was well-rehearsed.

"You knew when you signed on that wasn't an option." He was right, though. There wasn't much more he could do for her, not since the organization knew. All except Black and Monday, anyway.

Like the light of a new day, an idea dawned in her mind.

"I know, I know," he was saying. He kept pleading his case, but she wasn't really listening. Her eyes rested on him, giving him the impression he had her attention, but the wheels turned in her mind as she constructed the details of his new purpose. She would kill Silver for even asking, and save quite a bit on the budget in doing so. But – just maybe – Silver could hold the key to breaking Black entirely.

"Alright," she said, interrupting the old man's ramblings. "Come with me." She closed the drawer which held the button to the door, along with a few others. One would send gas into the lower floor, making everyone there fall asleep. She didn't want to kill her experiments, so it wouldn't do any permanent harm. A second button would flush the area so she could send in a collection team.

Those buttons would be reserved, though. She would kill Silver the old-fashioned way – in a way a self-made man like himself might appreciate. Had her victim been Monday or Black, she would probably have not risked closing the distance and used a gun. But Silver was old and guns were loud. For this, she would use a knife. "Tell me again when they planned to attack?" she ordered more than asked as she stood and led him to the door.

Silver was quick, eager even, to obey, following her like a puppy. "Tomorrow," he answered, "Probably in the afternoon, because Blue will be off and available around that time." She knew and remembered all of this, but getting the old man to talk was easy and kept him distracted as they walked. She even managed to pick up one of the knives on display in her office on the way out without him noticing.

They ran into the indoor patrol in the hall to the elevator. The men scuttled away quickly enough, sure to stay out from under Natasha's feet. They were well-trained mice, to be sure.

Natasha waited - patiently, in her opinion - in the elevator as Silver rambled on. She didn't really care if he noticed her absentmindedness, so long as he didn't notice the blade and force her to spoil the surprise for Black.

There were two doors outside Black's cell. One led to within his interrogation chamber, and the other to the observation room. A panel between them held two switches. One lit Black's room, which was still set to "off" since Monday's torturing. The other, if turned on, would reverse the one-way mirror effect and the occupant of the cell would be able to see into the control room. In this case, that was exactly what she wanted. She flicked that light on as she passed it, holding the door open for Silver to walk in first. He had quieted sometime during their walk and moved into the room slowly but without protest. Natasha followed, closing the door behind her.

Silver stared into the blackness that was the window. "What am I doing here? Is my money – "

Natasha sighed, exhausted by his rambling. She reached her blade across his wrinkled throat and pulled. Blood flooded over the line she had drawn through the skin

and muscle, killing him nearly instantly, only giving him time
to shut up and maybe raise an eyebrow in surprise.

A glance at the heat monitors told her Black was back
in his corner. She stared into the darkness at where he would
be as Silver fell under his own weight. Natasha counted to
ten, maintaining the stare, before turning and walking out,
leaving the body there and flicking both switches on her way.

Cyan got a text after about an hour of wandering
about the grounds of his house. Even the sunset was less
appealing than normal today. Nothing would be until his
friends accepted him again and he knew White was alright.
Silver's death weighed on him, too. What if he had been
there? Could his presence have kept Silver from having to
defend White? If he returned sooner, would Silver be still
alive? Breanne could have waited in the back of Green's car a
little longer without any different results.

The backyard wasn't exactly wilderness, but the
accepting calmness of the area soothed him slightly. A
chipmunk even watched him as he walked. They made eye
contact for a full twenty seconds. That was when the text
arrived. The chime seemed loud in the stillness, and the critter
dashed away, the sound surprising it, too.

Cyan pulled his phone out, eager for news. All the
text contained was an address. He knew the street. It was on
the east side of town. The text had come from Saturday,
however, a fact which made Cyan's hope soar. It must be the
address for their new base of operations, but it meant so
much more. It meant White was back and they had been
convinced of the truth of his innocence. Cyan patted his
pocket, where Green's phone still rested, and started back
toward his home.

What about Breanne? His steps faltered as he
climbed the gentle hill. Could he leave her alone again at a
time like this? From where he stood, he could see the light in

her second story bedroom window. She was lying on her bed, propping the diary up with her left hand as she wrote feverishly with her right. The stream of thought to paper stopped only to wipe away a tear. She would be fine.

On his way back home, he spoke with his groundskeeper and asked that they bring her a hot cider, Breanne's favorite and most comforting drink, in about half an hour. They said they'd be happy to, so Cyan headed out.

He was at the end of the driveway when his phone chimed again, this time from Scarlett. *Pick us up at the pool.* There was no swimming pool in town, at least to his knowledge, so she must mean the pool hall.

Us? he texted back.

I've been drinking and Green didn't come by himself. Unless you want Green to drive your Porsche...

Scarlett didn't need to finish the sentence. Cyan was only grateful he was already in his BMW.

On my way.

Green saw Scarlett nod to him. To anyone else, it would appear that they were flirting, but Green knew it meant their ride was coming.

"Hey!" Fischer called to him, stepping between Green and Scarlett. Green was getting bored of this verbal tug-of-war with the man, but didn't know how exactly to avoid it. "She's mine, man. We had a deal." The deal, in Green's opinion, was off as soon as Fischer had thrown that first punch.

Green just grunted, turning his back on the man to bend down to the green felt and shoot. The movement shunned Fischer, making him look bad in front of the rest of the crew. Fischer dropped the subject, but still shot hostile glances as they continued their game.

By the time they reached the end of the game, Scarlett had moved between them, taunting. "Winner gets a kiss," she said. Green glanced up in time to see her bite her lip. For a moment Green forgot himself, consumed by just how attractive she really was.

It was just the cue ball and the eight ball on the table, and Fischer's turn. Green hoped to win just to wipe that smug look off the man's face. Fischer shot, but with too much gusto. The eight ball went next to the pocket and rattled back and forth in front of it before coming to a stop directly in line for Green to land.

Fischer sent a look to Green, warning him to lose. Green knew exactly how to, if any trace in him had wanted to. Instead, he just leaned down, letting himself smile. With all the delicacy and finesse that Fischer had lacked – which Green admittedly used only exclusively for playing pool – he struck. The cue ball glided gently across the table and just kissed the black eight ball, coaxing it in.

Green looked up and smiled back at Fischer, but the man would have none of it. Without a word, the man swung his pool cue.

Green had two options to avoid the stick-turned-weapon. He could dodge it by going down and cowering beneath the pool table, or he could close the distance, making the cue unwieldy and entirely useless as a weapon. The latter was the obvious choice.

As he stepped in, Green threw his left hand out at Fischer's arm. It landed before the cue could come around to him, and he stared Fischer down instead of continuing the fight. The blow was just enough to release Fischer's grip on the cue, and Green heard it clatter onto the felt behind him. Fischer glared at him, clearly defeated again, but not yet willing to give up. Green gladly held his gaze.

The door slammed open behind him and Fischer's gaze moved from stubbornness toward Green to surprise and fear at the newcomer. Green turned to see Cyan storm in, immediately commanding the attention of the room.

"That's him! That's the guy!" one of the agents behind Green whispered.

Cyan's shoulders were rolled forward, making him appear larger and stronger than the Cyan he knew. He glared at the group of them from the tops of his eyes, cracking his neck as he wrapped his arm around Scarlett, who went with him easily.

Green had to admit – had he not known Cyan, he would have been intimidated.

But Cyan was an actor, not a fighter. "Any of you trying to steal my girl?" he asked.

Green looked to Fischer, who had clearly been the one flirting with Scarlett all night, but he, along with most of the others Green could see, all pointed back at him.

Cyan lunged at Green, ferocious, and grabbed his t-shirt by the fistful. "Work with me," Cyan whispered so only they could hear. Right.

Green gradually pushed himself upward, until he stood on his toes. Cyan played along, giving the appearance that he had lifted Green up by his shirt.

Then Cyan did something unexpected. He rocked his shoulders. When it came to interpreting thoughts and ideas, Green had no clue how to read people. But when it came to what they would do with their limbs next, Green's insight's rarely failed him. In this case, he could tell Cyan meant to throw him. To avoid such a fate, the solution was as simple as just planting his feet and bracing for it against someone as light as Cyan. In this case, though, he would follow whatever plan Cyan had created.

Green threw himself on the floor between two tables, landing harmlessly on his shoulder before turning face down. He could hear Cyan's angry steps approach and did nothing to stop them. He felt a tug on his collar again, this time from the back, prompting him to rise to his knees, as if pulled up.

"No fighting allowed," came the loud but surprisingly bored shout from the bartender.

"Then we'll take this outside," Cyan said through gritted teeth. "Come on, babe."

Scarlett pattered after them as they left, letting the door close behind them before Cyan released his collar and smiled.

"Nice acting back there," Green said as he flattened his t-shirt, old though it was.

"Like it? I was channeling my inner Green." Cyan lifted the corner of his lip in a snarl worthy of a Disney villain, and they all shared a laugh. "Thanks for working with me."

"Any time."

16

The screaming had stopped hours ago, but it still echoed through Black's skull. Even the buzzing, which was louder than ever, couldn't drown it out. Black stared, haunted by the sounds and the brutal display by Mother afterward. Why Silver? He was harmless! Cyan, he could understand. He was closer to a real threat. Green even. But Silver? He didn't even fight back, not that he would have won.

No matter what Black did, how he plugged his ears and squeezed his eyes closed, he couldn't block the images or sounds from his memory.

What could have happened at the organization to put the kindly man in her clutches? Had she found the organization's headquarters and raided them? Fear rippled through Black. Fear that history had repeated itself. Fear that once again Black was at fault for another death within the organization. Fear that they had acted too soon and come to ruin. Fear that harm had come to Saturday – the only person left who both knew Black's entire dark history and accepted him anyway.

With the organization out of the picture, Black was trapped. Helpless.

So, Black stared. Part of him hoped his brother had finally died in the end. No one should have to endure even the memory of that kind of pain. But, had he died, Black would never have the chance to tell him he was sorry for putting him in that position and that he had joined the organization to continue his work. He would never know he would be proud of the man Black was now. As he thought it, even the concept of that conversation seemed absurd.

What could Black do? Nothing.

Nothing he has done, or could ever do, would matter in the end. His once-steady hands now shook unless clenched, and he couldn't keep his thoughts in one spot longer than ten seconds.

The only anchor in his life was Mother. She was the sole constant, if only in that she was constantly evil. Dependably so. That counted for something, right?

I watched as the remaining organization members filed into the dining room of the rather large home. Limey worked feverishly on his laptop. He had cracked a code in Green's pictures, whatever that meant. Blue came in, wearing a polo very similar to his uniform, immediately filling the room with comfort and protection. I had only ever spoken to Gold and Red during my interview process earlier that day, but I was glad they were there, too. Saturday had told me that Tuesday had requested Lavendar after I had spoken to him, and the cook had been sent off to join him in Phoenix. As Orange entered, he angled directly for me.

"Your apartment is back to normal," he said. "I'm sorry about your dog."

Lucy. A lump rose in my throat at the memory. "What did you do with her?" I asked, somewhat afraid of the answer. She was a good dog in life. The best. She deserved a good funeral, not to just be thrown away.

"Cremated her," he answered. I supposed that was better than rotting in the ground. "I put her ashes in the rose bushes outside your apartment," he continued, clearly eager to comfort me. "She'll be helping make the world more beautiful again, see? Even when dead." He was frank, but I appreciated that about him.

"Thank you," was all I could say, momentarily overwhelmed by emotion. It was a fitting end for my girl. I saw, on the edge of my vision, Orange reach out, as if to comfort me. He must have thought better of it, though, and let his hand fall before it touched my shoulder.

I collected myself with a deep breath. This was not the time nor place to mourn her. A glance around showed we were still missing Green, Cyan, and Scarlett. Neither Black nor Silver would be there, of course. But they, in very different ways, were why we were gathering in the first place.

Saturday was busy setting up the projector when the last three members came in together. I stood and leaned over the table, picking up where our leader had left off when he turned to address them. I wasn't nearly up to Limey's abilities with technology, but I had a certain affinity for it. Projectors, like cameras and TV screens, weren't hard to figure out. They just needed power and input.

Chatter filled the room as the last of the group they expected had entered. Many were welcoming Cyan back. Limey thanked Green for the pictures and got more from him to decode. Red and Gold hadn't really stopped their conversation since before I had entered. Orange gave Scarlett an awkward but welcoming hug before flitting away, head down and cheeks flushed.

I pushed the button on the projector, powering it on. Once he noticed, Saturday clapped his hands twice, collecting the attention of everyone in the room. The projector threw blue onto the whiteboard, with white numbers counting down in the middle until it was ready.

Everyone, myself included, sat down and quieted. Saturday stood and flicked the lights off. "We have an interesting problem before us," he started. "Black is expecting us to come get him tomorrow. Silver's unfortunate betrayal also tells us that they know we're coming to get him. We've all had a long day, and as much as I know we want to go after him as soon as possible, we all need to be well-rested if this is going to work."

"Can we tell Silver we've pushed it back to Wednesday? Feed them false information?" Gold asked.

"As far as we can tell," Saturday answered, glancing at Blue, "he's in the wind. I'd love to, if we could contact him and convince him to trust us, but I don't think we can depend on that."

Gold nodded, understanding. As I glanced about the room, no other ideas arose.

"My shift there starts at eight a.m.," Green said. "If you want to use me, it'd probably have to be after that, though they do demand we bunk there for the night."

"My shift at the station starts at nine. If you need me here, though, I can take some personal time." Blue's face was sympathetic but stoic. I could tell everyone here was ready to sacrifice nearly everything in order to bring Black home safely. But I also knew it wouldn't mean anything if another got captured or killed in his stead.

"We may actually want you on duty for this one, Blue." Saturday spoke with authority, gently commanding the attention of the room. "One of my concerns is containment. We need to make sure we take as much advantage away from them as possible. That means limiting outside intervention, either from the police or the senator, assuming he's not there."

"Done," Blue said, leaning back.

"You can do that?" I asked before I could stop myself. I didn't realize, however decorated an officer he was, he could command them to ignore a call for help.

"I'll trade patrols. I don't really need to be downtown as much anymore anyway." Blue looked around the house, located on the other side of town. I understood. "Then, if dispatch gets a call for help, I'll make sure I can be the one who gets sent." It made perfect sense.

"What about the senator?" Cyan asked. "White? Can you tell us anything about him that we can use?"

"He can't keep it in his pants," I said without hesitation or regard for Lewitt's dignity, remembering Liza's story.

"I'll make sure he's distracted, then," Scarlett said. It was a disturbing thought to me, but she didn't seem to mind in the least.

"Then we have containment," Cyan said.

"Good." Somber though he had looked all evening, Saturday now also looked proud.

Suddenly the blue hue throughout the room changed to white, drawing my attention to what Limey had sent through the projector, with his laptop.

It was a map showing what I suspected to be two floors of one building. One floor was U-shaped, while the other was missing a wing, so it looked more like an L.

"This, plus a little more, is what I've put together from the info Green got to us." Limey looked quite pleased with himself.

"A map?" Red asked.

"It would seem so, though I don't understand the locations."

"You mentioned a little more?" Saturday asked.

"Stuff about their computer network security. Useful, but not really interesting if you want me to explain it."

"I want you to hack it. Can you?" Saturday asked.

"That would definitely be helpful," Cyan added.

"I can try. It would be easier if I could be there, though."

"What if you were there virtually?" I asked. I remembered that corporate could, whenever they needed to, take over my computer at work. Mostly it was used as a long-distance IT, but the concept would be useful in this case.

"It's a closed network, I guarantee it. I'd need to make a hole to get in, but I need to be in to make a hole.

That's their primary security system." Hm. I had no solution there.

"Could Green help create a hole for you?" Saturday asked. "Seeing as he's already accepted on the inside."

I could hear Cyan's snort of skepticism, but Limey didn't appear to immediately reject the idea. I thought he would have dismissed the suggestion out of hand, as Green's strengths did not exactly lie with technology. An image of Green hacking into a secure government server was amusing at best.

"That's an option," Limey said. What was he thinking?

"I should warn you…" Green started.

"Can you get near a computer?" Limey interrupted.

The information he'd provided earlier proved that was possible. "Yes."

"You know what a USB drive looks like?"

A pause. "Yes. I think so."

"At the end of the night, I'll give you a USB drive. All I need you to do is put it in one of the computers. Then I can access it via VPN." Green had a blank look on his face, but I mostly followed. The idea just might work. "Once inside, I could access basically whatever I wanted."

"Could you turn off alarms and change security passwords?" Saturday asked. I understood his line of thinking. The farther we could get in without raising an alarm, the more likely we were to make a clean getaway. Suddenly I felt like I was living in a heist movie.

"I don't know how much I can change things without raising suspicion. It depends on their people and how skilled they are with tech. I would only feel safe adding new information, not overriding or changing anything already existing."

"Can you add people into their system?" Cyan asked.

"How do you mean?" Limey asked. "Do you want to hack in, too?"

"No, I mean add people to their roster." He touched the security card around Green's neck.

"Oh! Sure, I don't see why not. I'll just copy the card Scarlett gave me yesterday."

"How long will that take?" Saturday asked.

"Depending on how many, I could be done by tomorrow morning. I could use an extra pair of hands, though. Red?" Limey asked. The Brit was the youngest of the group around me, but seemed comfortable with asking for help.

"Happily."

"Good. As far as how many, that's to be determined next," Saturday started.

"I'm going in," Cyan said immediately.

"We may need you as a driver after –" Saturday's face was full of concern, but Cyan's of determination.

"I'll do that too, but I'm going in. This is personal. They made it personal when they took Breanne. I want to be front and center in taking them down."

I understood his feelings completely, but didn't agree he should go in when he was so riled up. Emotions could either cloud or hone judgment, depending on the person. It was a risky call, but fortunately not mine to make.

"Okay," Saturday said after a moment. "But you follow my command. To the T."

Cyan nodded. "I had no intentions otherwise."

"How about this," Saturday proposed. "Cyan, Orange, Gold and myself go inside. We'll meet with Green once in. Then Orange and Gold, you two stay in the cars while Cyan, Green, and I find Black. Does that work?" Nods around the room. "Four, then," he said to Limey.

"Tomorrow morning before nine, best guess," Limey responded. That seemed a suitable hour, considering the timeline thus far.

I couldn't help but notice I had not been involved in the plan. "What about me?" I asked. "What can I do?"

"I'm not sure going undercover is really your strong suit," Cyan said. He was right, of course. I was a terrible liar.

"Do you have any suggestions or ideas as to what you want to do?" Saturday asked.

As I looked around the room, I could tell everyone had their strengths and was able to contribute them in some way. What did I have?

I was a reporter. My weapon was a camera.

"All due respect, rescuing Black is one thing, but it won't stop the operation. What will prevent them from doing this again, but to someone we can't protect? We need evidence to stop them."

"What do you propose?" Saturday asked again.

I answered as the idea was still coming to me. "I have cameras galore at my apartment. We need evidence of what's going on there. Just having us as witnesses might not be enough. We could attach cameras to you and your vehicles. If we could capture everything inside and out, we could expose them."

"She's right," Gold said. "Video is invaluable in the court of law."

"I can also feed her the cameras on the compound," Limey volunteered.

"I'll be the eyes in the sky, then," I suggested.

Saturday nodded his approval.

I sat back in my chair, contented with my task. This was why I had become a reporter: to make a difference. I was going to be able to right wrongs without fighting or harming anyone. Except those who deserved it. But, in reality, they were the ones harming themselves. I was just the one that would introduce them to justice.

Scarlett was actually looking forward to her task. The sex was generally all the same, but the joy was in the power she would hold over him in deceiving him, and any blackmail that could come. She had never held control over anyone as powerful as a senator, though.

Charming security grunts at the pool hall was one thing, but Lewitt would be something else entirely. In the time it took Scarlett to pick out the right dress - a formal gown with a lot of slink - and do her hair, Limey and White had researched where the senator was scheduled to be that evening. He had a 9 o'clock reservation at the fancy outdoor Italian restaurant in town, therefore so did she. The reservation they set up was for two, though Scarlett had no plans to bring someone with her. She had a ruse in mind, and by 8:45 that evening, she was ready to execute it.

"You look stunning," Blue said as he opened the door to his car for her.

"Thank you," she responded as she sat, though "that's the idea" was the phrase more accurately running through her mind. Blue was giving her a ride to the restaurant-hotel. He didn't live too far away, so if things got hairy, she could always call him.

The ride was brief, and before long they were at the drop-off/valet parking. With a "Good luck!" from Blue, she stepped out of the car and into the lobby. To her right was the restaurant, and to the left was the attached hotel. Perfect.

She gave her name and was seated outside. The summer air was crisp but comfortable. A man sang over the speakers in Italian, fitting the restaurant theme. Were Black with her, she'd probably ask him to translate the lyrics. It didn't really matter anyway. Getting that man to talk was an effort in itself.

Scarlett's table was set with two glasses of water and two wine glasses, yet to be filled. There were even candles on the table. Not long after, the Senator was also seated a few tables away. Scarlett moved her chair slightly but subtly so that she was sitting entirely in the light provided by the restaurant and the candles.

The waiter had offered him a seat facing away from Scarlett, but he intentionally chose the other side, facing her. Good. She had already gotten his attention.

Scarlett let fifteen minutes go by, visibly checking the time on her phone and looking around. After appearing suitably anxious, she shot a text to Cyan saying she was ready. The plan was for him to call the restaurant and tell them he wasn't coming. If the senator was looking, and she was reasonably sure he would be, he could ask the restaurant what happened. Once word got to him that she was alone for the night, the rest would be easy.

The plan worked perfectly. The waiter came by and told her about Cyan's phone call, and the senator was staring the whole time. The waiter left, bringing one of the water and one of the wine glasses with him, a clear indication she was stood up, just in case the senator needed one.

Seconds went by, then minutes. What was taking him so long? Hadn't he noticed? Scarlett pulled the pin from her hair, letting her wavy blonde locks roll down her shoulder.

That had grabbed his attention. Scarlett saw in her peripheral vision the senator stop one of the restaurant staff and ask about what had happened, nod, then wait for the man to leave before coming over to Scarlett. Finally!

Scarlett kept her head down, letting her hair hide her face and trying to appear demure and vulnerable. "Is everything alright, miss?" he asked.

"Red blend, please," she said, affecting a tear-struck voice and handing him the wine glass without looking.

"I'm not the waiter."

She looked up, pretending to notice him for the first time. "Oh! I'm so sorry! So stupid of me!"

"I'll make sure the waiter knows next time he comes around, though."

She took the glass back from him hastily and set it down. "I'm so sorry. Where are my manners? Please, sit with me?"

"The seat's not taken?" the man asked, sitting anyway.

"Not anymore. He stood me up. I can't believe, after last night, he would just —" Scarlett pretended to catch herself. "You don't want to hear about him. I'm sorry."

"He's a complete idiot if he let a beautiful woman like you get away."

"I don't look beautiful now," she said, wiping away the only real tear she had managed.

"You're welcome to go and wash up if it'll make you feel better." Somehow, if she were sincere, that was the last thing Scarlett would have wanted to hear. Fortunately for the senator, she wasn't.

"I don't have a room here," she said, knowing exactly how he would answer next.

"I do." He hadn't even offered her a name, nor asked one.

She forced a smile at him. "I'm not so sure I should," she said. Too easy and she'd lose him. "At least not without that bottle of wine."

"That can be arranged." It was like she didn't even have to try.

Green felt like he was back in junior college, sneaking back into the dorms after a night of mischief-making. It was nearly midnight by the time he had returned. Many of the men were still awake, and, if he was honest with himself, he was too wound up to rest, as Saturday insisted.

Once they figured out everyone's main jobs, the rest of the meeting was spent with Saturday laying out the details of the plan, with additions from Green about operations at the government compound. After that, being back at the base and sneaking to bed just felt odd, like being guilty of some sort of crime, except Green did not regret anything he had said or done. Maybe more like being under a microscope, he decided, though the government had no reason to suspect him.

White had offered to use her TV makeup skills to give him a fake bruise to maintain his cover, but he had declined. If they discovered it was makeup – and they inevitably would – then his cover would be blown entirely. He could just tell them he had escaped Cyan's wrath once outside and walked back to the compound. Hopefully, though, no one would ask.

The USB drive Limey had given him weighed heavily in his pocket; it was much heavier than any scale would tell him. The whole plan, when it came to getting in and out again, hinged on him getting the drive into a computer. No computer access meant the crew couldn't get in. Without them, Black was left on the lower level of this compound alone and Green would likely be dead by this time tomorrow.

Green sat up on his cot. He couldn't stand it any longer. He would not be able to rest until the drive was out of his pocket and in a computer.

Sneaking around the night patrol was predictably easy. He found the same office he'd visited earlier. It was again empty.

He pulled the drive out of his pocket and, the room being lit by only the moon through the window, tried to find a hole on the computer tower under the desk that matched the drive. He thought he spied one in the front, but when he tried, it didn't go all the way in. So he looked at the back, climbing under the desk entirely, and using the pink cell phone as a light.

It was then that he heard footsteps walk by the room. Green held his breath and froze. Why had he left the door open? The footsteps paused, closed the door, then continued on the other side down the hall the other way.

As soon as he heard them retreat, he released his breath slowly. That was closer than he was comfortable with. He had no plan if he had been caught. No story prepared.

He would be glad when this was over.

With the aid of the pink flashlight, Green found a vertical slot that also matched the thing he had in his hand. He didn't recall Limey saying anything about the slot being vertical, but whatever. He didn't understand most of what came out of that man's mouth.

The metal piece clicked into place. Finally. Once the computer booted up the next morning, the thing would connect and Limey would be in. Green heaved a sigh of relief. He would finally be able to sleep.

Tuesday

17

Cyan woke the next morning before dawn. His first thought was concern for his sister. The second was about the mission. He quietly threw some pajamas on and tread down the hall barefoot until he got to his sister's room. He pushed on the door, half expecting her to be gone, but she was snoozing, safe and sound. Of course she was asleep. He gently pulled the door closed again and went back to his room. School wasn't even an option after yesterday.

Instead of following his sister's lead, Cyan got dressed. It was late enough that anyone who spotted him would just think he was up early.

The sun was just rising as he snuck down stairs and out the door.

"Who's there?" a strong male voice called suddenly as Cyan started to close it. The light flicked on in the foyer.

Cyan stepped back through the door and showed his face, putting a finger to his lips and pointing upstairs. His butler understood: Breanne was still sleeping.

"Why are you up so early?" he asked Cyan in a checked tone. "If you don't mind me asking."

"I couldn't sleep. I might ask the same of you," Cyan responded.

"Not a wink. Not after what happened yesterday." Cyan understood. The man had helped raise Breanne. The girl had shared her story with the staff, naming Green as her savior, but they all remained, for the time being, ignorant of the organization.

"I'm heading out to get some coffee," Cyan told him, only half true. His assigned task to get ready for the day was to get an untraceable vehicle. The coffee was just an added bonus and gave him something to do. "Can I bring you some?" Cyan offered.

The man waved his hand. "I can make some here." Cyan had expected as much. The staff had access to anything they wanted in the kitchen. Once a maid had been caught stealing chocolates. When the butler informed him about it, Cyan told him it was now the butler's responsibility to make sure there were always chocolates kept in that same place for her.

"Okay then." Cyan waved a farewell and stepped back out the door and chose a car.

I woke up with Orange standing over me. I had slept on the couch at the new base of operations after Cyan had insisted my apartment wouldn't be safe until after the strike. I also had a blanket on me I didn't remember grabbing.

Startled by Orange's presence, I pulled the blanket close as I sat up. "What is it? Is everything okay?" I asked, wiping the sleepiness from my eyes.

"Sorry, sorry!" The man put his hands up in a gesture of surrender. "I brought your cameras for you, but I didn't know if I should wake you or not."

"It's fine. I'm up now." I let the blanket drop, though I was still being watched. "Thank you," I said, trying to politely indicate that he could go.

The small man jumped, startled in his own right, and scampered off with an "Oh!"

Cyan must have heard the commotion from the other room and came in, nearly being knocked over by Orange in the process. Cyan laughed, dancing with hands full of paper cups from the local coffee shop as he stepped out of the way.

"He's an odd one, isn't he?" I asked Cyan as he sat on the couch next to me, handing me one of the cups.

"Two creams, three sugars?" Perfect. "He's just a little intimidated by the female species as a whole. Brilliant mind, though it works completely differently than most."

"Intimidated and fascinated, apparently," I corrected with a smile.

"You kind of have to treat him like a pet. At least, that's how Scarlett handles it." We shared a laugh before I sipped the coffee. It was still a little too hot. "You ready for today?"

"I think so," I answered honestly. "My part isn't that hard. You?"

"I'm ready for this to be over. I can't look at my sister knowing those people are still out there." He heaved a sigh and sipped his coffee.

"We'll get them," I assured him. "How much will you tell her?" If I were in his position, I wouldn't know how to answer the question.

"I'm kind of hoping she won't ask. She knows she can tell me anything, and that I won't lie to her if she asks. But she's too young to be involved in something like this. Her biggest worries should be school and boys. Not this."

I had to agree. This would only contaminate her ability to focus on school. "Well, if she needs someone," I hesitated, trying to choose my words carefully, not wanting to offend him, "female to talk to, I'm here."

He smiled understandingly, patting me on the shoulder. "Thank you. How long will it take to rig the cameras?" he asked, changing pace.

"Not long." I sifted through the bag Orange had delivered and found one that slides into a shirt pocket. I glanced at Cyan, making sure he had one. As he had every time I had seen him, he was wearing a button-up shirt with a pocket. "Take this one. The power button is here, and the red circle records. The battery dies kind of quickly, though, so start it last minute." I slipped it into his hand. "Just put it in your pocket facing out. Yours is the only one that records decent audio." I was talking too much and I knew it.

He dropped it in his pocket comfortably. It looked like a smartphone there. "Got it." He smiled confidently at me.

Saturday was the only other one who would wear a camera. The others would have them mounted within their cars. "Can you get Saturday when he's ready?" I asked.

"Sure. You said I can use my Bluetooth?"

Right. Everyone on the team was to be equipped with a Bluetooth earpiece so we could conference call each other. I was going to be the one communicating to them what I saw, when needed. "Yes, it'll do. Call me when you get out there."

"Understood." Cyan stood up and trotted out, stopping halfway and coming back for his coffee before continuing out.

In the time it took me to find and prepare the bulkier camera that was to be Saturday's, Cyan had communicated my request for him. This camera was about half the size of my fist, but waterproof and it could be turned on remotely.

"White?" Saturday turned the corner and poked his head into the living room. "We're nearly set. How are you doing?"

"Just need to rig you up with this." I held the camera aloft. He stepped over and sat obediently, like a schoolgirl expecting to get her hair done. I had a chest harness for it, but it wouldn't work with the gun holster he was already wearing. Maybe I could combine them? I pulled the clips off my harness and attached them to his, making sure it would hold the camera's weight. "Is that comfortable? Balanced?" I asked.

Saturday rolled his shoulders. "Feels good."

"Good." I left the clips on the holster but took the camera away. "It's too obvious until you get past security. Once you're in, just clip it into place. Make sense?"

"How do I turn it on?" he asked, taking the camera from me.

"I'll take care of that remotely." I picked up a Bluetooth earpiece and handed it to him. "Take this, too."

Scarlett rolled over as she woke. The night was, to her surprise, not as terrible as she had expected. The senator knew what he wanted, a desirable trait in any other man. She had made an effort to keep him up late into the night, and he still slept now. As she rolled, she got a glimpse of the clock on her phone – 9:14. The strike was to take place at 9:26. She needed to guarantee he would not answer his phone during that time.

Scarlett swung her bare legs out of bed and stood, planning to determine just how deeply the man slept. The alarm clock that came with the room had been knocked over last night, and was somewhere under the bed at that moment. She pulled the curtains to the only window in the room, deceiving his internal clock into thinking it was still earlier than it was. Unfortunately, the curtains were louder in the morning stillness than they were in the flurry of last night.

"Hey," he cooed, waking slightly and looking at her.

Scarlett smiled softly at him. "Hey, yourself. I was hoping to keep it a little darker in here for you. You had a late night." She intentionally stood in a subtle but seductive pose, aware she was backlit by the mostly-closed curtains.

"Refresh my memory?" he asked, patting the bed sheets next to himself. It wasn't a particularly tempting offer when coming from the senator.

"I need a shower first." Scarlett balled up her hair and pulled her pin from the nightstand to keep her hair up, aware of how the posture made her body look to him.

Then she sauntered past the bed to the restroom as the man flopped back onto his pillow. He was still a man, though, and therefore under her control.

She stopped at the doorway, holding onto the trim, and looked at him. "I didn't say you couldn't join me."

Scarlett smiled as the man's eyes popped open again at her offer. Yes, she could definitely keep him away from his phone for the next twenty minutes.

Green glanced at his watch. Fortunately, his cover allowed for pacing and solitude. He was back on patrol outside, as he had been ordered. Everything had gone according to plan, at least to his knowledge. Had the USB drive thing worked? There was no knowing until he was long gone from this place.

The next ten minutes would be vital. He knew his part and what he had to do. Assuming every part of the plan ran perfectly, this would be an easy and relatively harmless operation. No more of Markham's agents were scheduled to die, at least.

Cyan had flipped when Green told them about the actual Mercer, though. Killing a man was bad enough, even in self-defense. But it was the knowledge that his sister had shared a car – unbeknownst to her – with a dead man that had really riled Cyan. Green stood by his decisions even now, though.

Green checked his watch again. Any minute now. He patrolled near enough to his car that he could see the traffic pass by. That was it. The black SUV that Cyan had gotten for the event. That was Green's cue.

"I've got some suspicious activity by the abandoned car," Green announced, adopting his *Mercer* voice once again.

"Copy. Check it out."

"I'm working on it."

Green approached the car and walked around it, tracing Mercer's steps not twenty-four hours ago. Once on the other side and out of sight from the snipers, Green opened up the door and dumped the equipment he had stolen from the man, along with any evidence from his cover identity, inside the car.

Then he found it: the matches Orange had left for him. There were also other boxes of who-knows-what in the back seat. Gas had been leaked and pooled underneath the vehicle, too.

Green stepped back, then into a drainage ditch on the opposite side of the road. Striking the match was the easy part. Throwing it and destroying his only possession of real value – besides his gun collection – was a little more difficult.

For Black, he reminded himself. Green sighed and tossed the match.

The burning gasoline gave Green plenty of time to crouch in the drainage ditch, but when the flames hit the mystery crates, he was glad he had. Orange was a weirdo, no doubt, but he knew his explosives.

The blast rocked the ground under Green's hiding spot, accompanied by a massive and loud boom. Debris flew over his head and across the ditch.

Green remained crouched until the boom had quelled into a constant, but still rather loud, roar of fire. If his understanding of the operations was accurate, they would send every man they could to investigate, leaving the front door more or less open to Saturday and the others. Fischer and his agents would find Mercer's body in the car and assume Green had died in the explosion. Dental records would even confirm it eventually, if it came to that.

Green was Green again. He allowed himself a contented sigh before popping his head back over the ditch. He had to be moving before the agents arrived. Onto the next step, then.

Cyan's security tag was under inspection when the sounds of the explosion reached them at the front gate. From his current position in the driver's seat, he couldn't see the car itself, but the black plume was already visible above the trees.

"What is that?" Cyan asked, pointing at the growing cloud, though it was impossible for anyone on the property to have missed the sound.

The man holding his badge shoved it back and waved at them to proceed. "Hurry!" he commanded. "We need all hands, ASAP!"

"Yes, sir!" Cyan snapped, pulling the car forward and through the checkpoint.

Saturday stared straight ahead from the passenger seat. "Good, good." Then he checked himself and started mounting the camera White had given him.

"Remind me not to get on Orange's bad side, eh?" Cyan said, joking loudly enough for everyone to hear. Hopefully the laughter would lower the stress levels some.

"No kidding," came White's voice in his ear. She could be heard by all of them, and was watching everything through the cameras. "Okay Cyan, turn the camera on now. I'm turning Saturday's on as well."

Right. Navigating the windy road with one hand, he reached into his pocket with the other and pushed the button on the side without pulling the whole piece out.

"Thank you." He got the impression White was doing something else as she spoke, but didn't ask what. For everyone but her, talking now officially was need-to-know only.

"Green checking in," came a new but familiar voice on the line.

"I hear you." All motherly affection from White was gone. She had her reporter voice, and probably posture, if

Cyan had to guess. "Okay Cyan, there's the last parking spot on the left. That'll put you by the doors."

Cyan didn't need to respond. She was tracking them and would know if he didn't understand just by watching.

Cyan spied the parking spot and backed in, not even turning off the car before hopping out. Gold quickly stepped up and filled the vacated driver's seat.

Technically Cyan was breaking the rules by letting anyone else drive. He had taken the car from a dealership for a "test drive" this morning, using his own Camaro as collateral, and would trade back once their mission was accomplished. Assuming everything went as planned. Then it would be difficult for the government to track down or to trace today's operation to the organization, at least.

Saturday got out as well, looking surprisingly comfortable in his gear. This was his show now, as Cyan had agreed. He would only take control if they ran into anyone unexpected and they needed Cyan to talk them out of it, which he would be more than happy to do. Talk only, Saturday had emphasized. Fighting wasn't Cyan's natural *métier* anyway.

"Looks like Green is headed your way." True to White's word, Green showed up on their left. Cyan stepped back as Saturday handed him a gun. Just a nod from the pile of muscle and they were moving forward again. "Elevator is on your right," White informed them as they entered.

The audacity of their plan – to enter first through the front gate, then through the front doors of the building – had initially struck Cyan as absurd. But with even the front lobby desk empty, he had to give it to Saturday and his planning skills.

The man turned right, leading Cyan and Green down the hall. "Wait!" came the voice in their ears, rather loudly. They all froze, but no one intruded on them.

"What is it?" Saturday asked.

"Into the bathrooms, now." Obedient, and uncomfortably blind to whatever White had detected, the small group ducked to their right again and waited. "A group of four just came up from the elevator," White explained after they took up the position.

Green shrugged at the number, but Cyan knew they couldn't risk being spotted. Not yet.

"All clear. Go."

Back into the hallway then. The elevator wasn't far. Once in, Saturday jammed the "close doors" button while Green hit the one for the lower floor. They were entirely in foreign territory now.

"Hold the doors!" came a shout from the other side.

Cyan looked to Saturday, who stalled, thinking. When it was clear the man would reach the doors before the elevator started moving, Saturday pushed them open again.

"Thanks." The agent stepped in and pushed the "close doors" button again.

Cyan saw Green and Saturday exchange glances, with the tiniest of nods from the latter.

Cyan only had time to back himself into a corner and out of the way before Green lunged at their intruder. He punched the newcomer in both kidneys at once, evoking a sound between a gasp and a yelp, partially in surprise, partially in pain. Simultaneously the agent arched his back. That must have been Green's plan, because that put the man's neck right at arm level for him. Quick as a viper, Green wrapped his elbow around the exposed neck and pulled it close.

Any further plans the agent had for noise-making were stifled as he struggled just to breathe.

Cyan watched in a sort of morbid fascination as Green did what he did best. Claws and flails struck Green, but Cyan's cohort showed a remarkable amount of patience for who he was. By the time the elevator doors opened, the agent had passed out. Cyan stepped aside as Saturday put two fingers on the agent's wrist, just to be sure. Saturday's nod told Cyan all he needed to know. He was out, but he would live.

The three stepped out of the elevator and looked around. Black was down here somewhere. It was just a matter of finding the right cell. That meant searching, one by one. Cyan looked to Saturday. He held his gaze only a moment before proceeding to the farthest, working their way back to the elevator.

18

"It's okay," Monday said to Black.

Mother had offered him another "treat", and this time Black had no choice but to accept. His brother stood before him, and all Black could do was stare. All those things he had wanted to say, all those feelings he had kept to himself for years, were gone. He couldn't think of any words at all. He couldn't even decide what to feel. He was just plain spent.

Black's analytical brain was having no trouble with the scene, however. The man opposite him had the same bone structure as his brother, but the face was scarred from more than just last night's events - it was mangled beyond seamless repair. Mother's work on him had been extensive.

Mother had not said it outright, but had made it clear with her tone of voice - and the fact she called Monday a treat - that she expected Black to kill him. Seeing him so damaged, Black wasn't so sure he shouldn't.

Mother had gone, but she had to be watching from the other side of the mirror.

Black stared at his big brother. The man he knew from his memory was lean and muscular, with a commanding presence. The Monday in front of him now just looked... weak. Frail, even. He hadn't seen the sun in years, judging by his pale skin. What he could see of the skin, anyway. Much of it was swollen where it had been burned. What wasn't twisted by fire had thin cuts scabbing across it, as if he had encountered a tattoo artist with a razor blade. The scabs swirled in loops, almost tribal in appearance, with the shapes and lines. All Mother's work, Black had no doubt. She had earned the cacophony of screams last night.

"It's okay," Monday said again. He knew what fate awaited him. There was no way he couldn't.

Actually doing the deed wouldn't be hard. Though Black was the younger brother, he had always been the better fighter. Their father had insisted they take Kung Fu classes from a young age, but Black had always shone brighter.

From where he stood, there were a hundred ways, at least, he could kill Monday in less than three seconds. Probably a strike to the jaw with his left fist, twisting the head awkwardly, followed by an upward strike to the jaw, popping the skull clean off the spine. Easy.

Yet, easy as it was, Black still hesitated. Most of him wasn't even sure what stalled him. It was what both Monday and Mother wanted, and at least Monday would finally be freed from this torment. Black could hardly blame him. He even envied Monday's fate, to some extent.

But however simple it would be, and however much they all wanted it, Black had trouble convincing himself to move.

His situation became a little easier as he thought of the girl he had seen days ago - no, yesterday - and what Mother would do if he didn't obey. He felt like the whole world was silently cheering him toward murdering his own brother. It was only a choice of how.

"It's alright." Monday moved toward Black.

They had stood, facing each other in the center of the room, for at least half an hour now. The instant Monday moved, Black recoiled. Monday insisted, though, until they were close enough to hear each other breathe.

Monday took Black's hands in his own, looking sadly at them, then to Black, and back. "I do not fault you. You have to survive. You have to beat this. Beat her. I'm okay. I love you." Then Monday did something completely unexpected. He placed Black's hands on his collarbone and stepped in, encouraging Black to choke him.

The war raged stronger, silent inside Black, half of himself begging his muscles to squeeze, the other half forbidding it. Black was sure the first half would win soon enough.

I paced, furiously watching the screens but unable to communicate. Saturday and his team were either too far underground or were blocked somehow once they had descended.

It didn't make sense! Black had placed a phone call from there, presumably. Cell service should have gone through! They must have some sort of controllable technology to block the feeds when needed, like when they're expecting an infiltration.

Even my ability to see through their cameras was cut off. I only hoped they were still recording. My only lens through which to see the sequence of events was the security cameras Limey had fed me.

I nearly pulled my hair out watching. I could see the group progressing slowly. Too slowly. Screen by screen and cell by cell, they searched. Far too many screens stood between Saturday and Black. I couldn't listen in, but I could tell that whatever was about to happen in Black's cell would not be good.

"Hurry up!" I shouted, though I knew it was useless.

"Calm yourself," Limey said patiently next to me as he typed away, leaning close to his computer.

I couldn't be calm, though. Black's hands rested around another man's neck. Neither I nor Limey was able to identify him, but he was surely another victim of Natasha Markham and Senator Lewitt. I glanced again to Saturday's group and found them in a room which showed signs of occupation, I assumed by the unknown man.

"Can I help?" Gold asked over the headset. In my frustration, I had forgotten he could still hear me. He had been silent the entire time.

"No," I commanded. By the time he got down there, they'd be at Black's cell. Everyone just needed to stick to their jobs. "Thanks, but they're on their own for now." It was easy enough to say, but it didn't make me feel any less useless with my communication down.

Green waited outside a cell, poised to be the first in, as Cyan pulled the door open. A cold burst of air was his first clue that this cell was different than the others. An obnoxiously loud buzzing was the second.

Green rushed in, gun up, and scanned the room left to right, assessing everything he saw. The room was blank, aside from a one-way mirror on the wall surrounded by cold steel. There were two occupants, besides Cyan and Saturday, who had filed in behind Green as he cleared the room.

The two men in the center of the room were both familiar, but wrong in many ways. The one standing was a nightmarish version of Black. What had they done to him? Nearly naked, he had his hands clenched around the throat of the other man, who knelt before him, covered in wounds. Green was slack-jawed for the moment it took to comprehend the distorted face of the kneeling man. Monday? He was alive?

"Black!" Cyan called, stepping forward to interrupt the murder-in-progress. "Stop! You don't have to do this!"

At those words, Black seemed to notice them for the first time. He dropped Monday, more out of surprise than answer to Cyan's words. Green watched Black scuttle backward, to the wall. The man behaved like a caged but very feral animal.

His eyes were what disturbed Green the most. His eyes were... dead. Swollen and red, yes, but that keen perceptiveness Green had always admired in the man was nowhere to be found.

Saturday lunged past Green as soon as Black let go. "Monday!" The moment he reached the collapsed man, Saturday patted his cheek, coaxing color and life to return. Green looked back to Black, who was standing with his back against the wall, arms spread out against it as if he was ready to push off and lunge at Saturday's back.

A loud crash interrupted the scene. Green spun, trying to identify its source. Cyan spun too, and they both saw what had caused the ruckus. The door had slammed shut. Cyan, who was closer, rushed to it, trying the handle, then turned to Green and shook his head. They were trapped.

A gentle, female voice overwhelmed the buzzing on the speakers. "Kill them, my pet," the motherly voice cooed. "Kill them all."

Green turned back to Black. He was the only one the voice could be addressing. But he wouldn't. Would he? She couldn't have turned him against the organization, not in just the two days he had been there.

The look in Black's eye surprised Green even more. Instead of breaking down and thanking them for coming to his rescue, Black's eyes actually flitted between the four men in the room with him. God, was he actually going to attack them?

Black's eyes settled on Saturday's back, the coldly logical target.

Green launched himself forward, reaching to intercept Black.

Then the lights went out.

How on earth had they gotten so far into the building? Natasha had heard no alarm, or really any warning signs. She had planned this whole thing, and now she had to leave, at her moment of triumph? Black was ready to prove himself to her – she knew it – then they showed up. How did they even get past the front gate without catching her attention?

As soon as she turned the lights off, she headed to the elevator. One of her men lay collapsed on the floor. No gun shot wound. They must have just knocked him out. Cowards.

"Get up," she spat, kicking him with the pointed toe of her high heel. The man rolled over but otherwise refused to move. Fine. She closed the elevator doors and waited as the cabin ascended back to the surface.

As soon as her phone got reception, Natasha started to dial. If her men were really as incompetent as they were proving themselves to be, she needed outside help. She needed Lewitt.

The phone rang seven times before going to voicemail. What on earth could draw him away from his phone so completely that he wouldn't answer when she called?

Fine. Locals would have to do.

"911, what is your emergency?" the calm female voice asked on the other side.

"There are some men here," Natasha gasped, adopting a victim's voice and tone. "I think they're going to hurt me!"

"Just stay calm, ma'am." Ma'am? Natasha wasn't that old. "I have your location as 1138 Plains Road. Is that accurate?"

"Yes. Hurry!" The elevator doors opened and Natasha stepped over the agent and into the hall, heading straight to her office, a plan forming even as she acted to the operator on the phone.

"I have an officer already dispatched to your location. Can I please get your name?"

"Oh god, they're going to find me! They're going to
–" Natasha hung up the phone, bored, as she entered her
office. She went straight to her desk and opened the drawer.
The narcotics she had in the air system of the lower level
were installed for exactly this purpose. She pressed the
button to release the gas, dialing Lewitt once again.

I froze when I saw Markham push her hand into a
drawer of her desk, palm up. What was she doing?
I thought I couldn't get more frustrated - and scared -
after the room that held my friends suddenly went dark.
Either the feed to the room that held the members of the
organization had been cut, or the lights had been turned off
and some unspeakable nightmare was happening within.
Both options were equally terrifying. Either way, I
wouldn't be able to help them. The ease with which Markham
approached the situation scared me the most. The evil
woman sat, proper but relaxed, stirring her steaming
beverage and watching her monitor. She looked like she
might just be reading some interesting article in her free time,
rather than sitting through an infiltration.
"What is she looking at?" I asked Limey, pushing the
microphone up and away from my mouth.
"Not now." The Brit typed furiously, eyes fixed on the
screen.
"What –"
"She did something to turn on the AC downstairs. We
need to counter it." Limey was now engaged in an invisible
battle of the minds. All I could do was hope that my side
would prove to be the winning side.
"Blue?" I called, pulling down my microphone. "How
far out are you?"
"Six minutes in this traffic." Too long. The only
people in range were Gold and Orange, and neither had a skill

set that could help them. Limey and I were down the street, but we had to maintain our posts to get the men out alive.

The lights turning off was like a slap in the face to Black. The dark had always been a cloak of protection for him. Now, it reminded him of who he really was. Before all this. How long had he been trapped in this room? He had no idea anymore.

Mother's order to "kill them" still rang in his ears. It would be easy now with the lights off. He knew exactly where everyone in the room stood - or knelt, in Saturday and Monday's case - and had heard no one move yet.

He had to obey. Hadn't he?

"Black," Cyan's voice cut through the darkness. True to Black's assumptions, the man hadn't moved. "It's us. We won't hurt you. Help us get you out of here. You and Monday." They were like the words of an angel. Or a demon disguised as one.

He had taken whatever pills Mother had offered him. The organization had abandoned him. The figures in front of him were figments of his imagination, then. Even Cyan's words must be generated by Black's own mind.

Then it all became clear to him.

This was a test. A test to see if he would obey Mother. And he hadn't failed yet.

Cyan heard the hiss of the ventilation before he smelled the air change. It was ultra-sweet, somewhere between foul fruit and the flavor of artificial sweetener. What were they pumping into the room?

He blinked in the darkness. Whatever it was he was smelling, Cyan knew it was only secondary to their primary threat: Black.

Cyan didn't know what he had expected when they came to get Black, but it wasn't this. He couldn't have turned against them. The Black Cyan knew was still in there, and he had to wake that man up again. But how?

Then a voice sliced through the darkness: Saturday. "Cyan, check the door again and talk to Black. Green, we need him alive or not at all. Black, stand down. We're here to help you."

Cyan almost didn't recognize the voice that answered. "The door's locked. It's always locked." Black. His voice was hoarse and hollow, but still echoed from the area he had retreated to before the lights turned off.

Cyan still moved back to where he thought the door had been, fumbling around in the dark until he found it. Locked, as expected.

Where was White? She should be there, on the phone, leading them through. He only hoped she and Limey hadn't been attacked.

Maybe she had just been cut off when they had come downstairs. Cyan comforted himself with the thought.

"We are real," Cyan said aloud, taking a wild stab at what Black might be thinking. "And we are here to help you." Cyan kept his back against the wall, as far from Black as possible. The buzzing had stopped with the lights, and the only noise in the room was the hiss of the air, and whatever Saturday was doing to Monday in the center to revive him. And Cyan's conversation with Black.

Green had either not moved or had moved silently. Knowing Green as he did, Cyan assumed the former. When it came to fights, Green was not exactly a subtle man. Black definitely had the upper hand here, in the dark, if it came to combat.

With a click, the ventilation shut off again. Limey. Their guardian angels had not forgotten them after all.

"It's off," I heard the Brit say.

I breathed a sigh of relief. Limey could do anything with that laptop. The fact that he had even detected the shift in AC still amazed me.

"Wonderful," I said, reaching over and patting him on the back without taking my eyes off the screen. "Communication next, please. Then lights, then the door."

"Got it."

Black and Cyan had conversed two days ago, when the former had first been taken captive. Therefore, reception down there was controlled to some extent, and chances were it had been digitally. Limey should be able to open communication up again.

Unfortunately, though, there was nothing we could do to help them with Black until then. Not from here.

Green remained motionless, listening to Cyan banter with Black, insisting that they were real. He would have to wait for Black to come attack him. Once he found Black's fist, he could find his elbow or throat or whatever Green wanted. Finding his own way to the feral man in the dark was an invitation to death's door, though.

At first he had been annoyed by Saturday stating the plan aloud like that. Not that he had any choice. White had been suspiciously silent since the elevator.

On second thought, by ordering Green to fight Black, Saturday had made Green the biggest target in the room. Black should attack him first, which was optimum. But it also meant that if Green was beaten, there was no real hope for the group as a whole.

"Have you moved, Green?" Black asked, suddenly breaking his conversation with Cyan.

Part of Green wanted to stay silent and make Black work for his answer. But Black knew where the others were, so if he couldn't find Green, he might attack them instead. "No," Green said aloud, reluctantly welcoming the fight and hoping beyond logic that he could do all Saturday asked of him.

Black heard Green's response and narrowed down his targets. He could tell the Army Ranger hadn't even shuffled his feet to face a different direction since the lights had turned off. Easy.

Like a swimmer launching from the side of a pool, he pushed off his wall, setting Saturday aside mentally and honing in on Green. Four steps and he was there, striking the side of Green's neck with his right arm, as if he were stabbing someone directly behind his target with an invisible ice pick. Black felt the neck simultaneously collapse and recoil as Green absorbed the blow.

What would he do next? They had sparred plenty of times before, but that all felt like a distant memory. He would elbow up, getting Black's arm in an awkward position if he left it there. So he didn't, instead pulling his right hand back to his core and swinging his left around to Green's back, anticipating his opponent would set his weight.

And he did, landing the small of his back right into Black's swinging fist. Green's grunt of pain was like music to Black's ears.

Then the man did something unexpected. He turned around, trying to face Black. That in itself wasn't particularly abnormal, but he swept Black's legs at the same time. Normally he stayed with his feet relatively planted, except when he would derive power from moving them. Rarely did he use them offensively.

It all went through Black's mind as he landed from Green's sweep, first on his rear and rolling down on his spine afterward, dispersing the force of the fall. The cold of the floor on his bare back didn't really bother him anymore.

If Green could keep him on the ground, he might actually stand a chance of beating him. Fortunately for Black, though, he was quicker and better at fighting blind. He rolled away, dodging a fist around his stomach as he did so.

Mother was right. This was kind of fun.

A treat.

19

Natasha watched the fight from her office upstairs, entranced. Before leaving, she had piped the imagery from the infrared cameras to her computer, so she could observe the scene as it played out even though her actors couldn't see a thing. Black was like lightning, twisting and dodging around Green. No, more like a sculptor as he worked.

It was almost a shame she had released the gas. Another minute or two, tops, and they would all be out cold. The fight was fascinating, while it lasted, at least.

Natasha was well aware of the chaos that happened among her peons outside her office door. Let them panic. She would deal with them later. The scene was contained, the culprits captured. They would be each put in separate cells, where she would work on them, too. Those that survived the next few minutes, at least. Everything, though unplanned, was in her control and running quite beautifully.

I went over everything I knew about the scenario and the compound in my head again as I watched the blank screen. Not only Green's account, but what Cyan had relayed from his sister's experiences.

That's when it clicked. She was the key. Could it be that the first person she said she had encountered there was Black? That seemed exactly like the kind of thing Markham would do to manipulate the organization's powerful members over to her side.

"Did Black ever meet Breanne before?" I asked the question aloud to anyone who could still hear me.

"I don't think so," and "No." Both responses came at the same time from Orange and Blue, respectively. Good enough for me.

"Thank you," I answered them.

"You'll be live again in five," Limey said, hitting a button on his laptop and counting down. Yes! "Two, one."

"Cyan!" I said immediately. He had to know. "Black was probably the guy Breanne met. Tell him she's safe."

Cyan's voice came over the headset, like music to my ears. "Black! That girl is safe. You don't have to do this. Markham can't harm her anymore."

The heavy breathing from Green's headset quieted.

Black had gotten her message.

"Her name is Breanne," Cyan said into the dark room. "She's my sister." What else could he say? The sounds of fighting had stopped, but Cyan had no clue how long the peace would last. "You're a good man, Black. My sister is alive because you and Green are both good men. She likes the color pink. Coral, she calls it. She's always wanted to see the northern lights and now, because of you, she can." What else? "Her favorite animal is a duck. That's why we don't have dogs – she wanted a pet duck instead."

"There's no way Mother would let her go free." Mother? He must mean Markham. She really had her claws dug deep in him, didn't she? Still, the statement told Cyan he was getting through to Black. Just not all the way yet.

"She thinks the girl is dead," Green said. "Markham thinks I killed her." Cyan heard the tussle between the two men start up again at those words.

How? How else could Cyan convince Black of the truth? It stared him right in the face and yet he chose to believe Markham's lies still. Cyan had his attention, but didn't know how to conclude.

Coughing and gasping filled the room from the center. Saturday had revived Monday!

A sigh of relief was audible from both Saturday and Cyan himself. How close that man had come to death's door, only Saturday would know. Cyan wondered, but would have to wait to ask. Then a loud thump sounded from somewhere further in the room. If Green was on the ground, in this darkness, then he had only seconds left before Black finished him off entirely. For the first time in his life, though, Cyan was at a loss for words.

Green was done for. He knew it before he had even hit the ground. Fighting Black under these circumstances was a foolish decision, to say the least. One that, if nothing changed soon, would end his life. Even still, he did not regret it. Crazily, Green's mother's voice flashed through his mind.

"Stubborn, stubborn boy. That'll get you killed some day. Mark my words. You'll die of stubbornness."

Green had protested at the time that he wouldn't, which, on looking back, Green realized had only proved her point.

Now, he lay on his back, catching his breath and waiting for Black to descend on him.

No. Not yet. He had to last just a little longer, until Saturday, Monday, and Cyan could get out.

Green pulled his knees up to his chest and rolled over, like a turtle going inside its shell, and just in time. He heard the slap of a fist hitting the ground where his throat had been moments before.

It was like Black could see where Green went. He kicked Green's side with enough strength to roll him back over. Like a monkey with a coconut, Black slammed the edge of his fist square on Green's forehead as he landed, swinging on Green's knees a moment later. Green was cracked open like a pill bug, face up. Again.

But this time, Black wouldn't let him cover up. Heel planted firmly on the ground, Black stepped onto Green's ankle and pressed, pushing the leg over awkwardly and evoking an unbidden yelp from Green. Painful though it was, it gave Green an idea how to find Black in the darkness. If that was Black's foot, then his leg had to be about...

Green sat up and lunged, wrapping his hand around to the inside of Black's thigh and grabbing as little skin as he could while maintaining a grip.

Black released a satisfying gasp of pain, quickly followed by a sound fist to the side of Green's head. And he was on the ground. Again.

He could feel Black's weight as he pounced on him once more, this time not bothering to keep his distance. Straddling Green, Black used his ankles to lock out Green's knees. Kicking or kneeing the feral man was now a useless strategy. Elbows rammed into the hollow spot beneath Green's collar bone, knocking the wind out of him once more. Fingertips found their way around the edges of Green's jaw bone, threatening to pull it off entirely.

"Black. Be still."

The words froze Green as well as his attacker. They sounded like Cyan's words, but in Black's own voice, from the direction of Saturday. Then Green understood.

Monday was the one speaking. "You're free to do what you will. Mother doesn't control you anymore. Her ammunition is gone. She can't harm you, or the girl. If you kill Green, it's of your own free will."

Silence reigned for a long time. The grip on Green's throat didn't even let him swallow. It was the moment of truth: Black would either believe them and be free with the organization again, or he would kill Green and fully succumb to Markham and her mania.

Then, silently, Green felt Black's grip on his jaw and knees lighten and fade away, as if Black were merely an apparition. Green stayed in his position, wondering if Monday's words had really had the effect Green wanted to believe they did.

No one dared to speak. Black moved back to his corner, trying to hide his emotions from them. What had he done?

These people were his friends, come to rescue him. And yet Black had wanted to kill them. Through and through, Black had been convinced they were the enemy.

Never had he been so wrong. That wasn't to say he was always right; he had done so many things he regretted in his past. But this... this was worse.

His world felt hot. He choked on the air as he sat down, crouched in his safe corner again. Every exhale brought the reality of what happened closer, until he broke.

He wept.

He didn't even fight it. He felt the liquid roll like fire across his face. A pressure built behind his nose that seemed to convince the tears they had to come out in full force. One sob, then another. He freely admitted to himself he was crying, the only sound made in the room. Even the sound of Mother's buzzing had ceased.

Not Mother. Markham. Natasha Markham.

It wasn't self pity that moved him – not exactly. More like self-loathing. He had fought his friends, the only ones in the world who cared about him in the least. And for what? Markham's approval? He scoffed at the thought, inadvertently blowing tears off the tip of his nose.

Black felt a touch on his shoulder and opened his eyes. The lights had turned on again. His big brother was there, gaze warm and pitiful. Behind him, Saturday, Green and Cyan stood, all staring at him. Black's face burned with shame. Not at the tears, but at his own deeds.

"It's okay." His brother's words were like warm honey on a sore throat. "We care about you. We forgive you. We love you."

Love him? The tears came fresh and hot. Black knew beyond a doubt he deserved the farthest thing from love. He felt more than saw his brother embrace him, and Black welcomed it. He even leaned in, burying his face in the comforting and long-missed familial shoulder.

I tore my eyes away from the screen that held the reunion scene, wiping tears of my own away. Blue had arrived in his patrol car and was awaiting instructions from me.

"Time to go, Saturday," I said. "Blue, arrest Markham. She's in her office."

Through the security cameras, I saw Blue hop out of his car and enter through the same way Saturday's team had minutes earlier. Blue crossed the elevator at the same time the other group rose and exited it.

Saturday was carrying Monday on his shoulder, and Cyan likewise for Black. Green was favoring his ankle but was otherwise walking fine on his own. With a nod, the sides separated again.

I watched with a sigh of relief as the group loaded into the SUV.

Natasha threw the phone across the room in anger. Why wasn't Lewitt answering? The phone separated from the battery as it collided with the wall before scattering its pieces across the carpet.

A moment later a knock came at the door. Finally! The senator must be here. "Natasha Markham?" That didn't sound like him. "Police, open up."

Natasha rushed to the door and opened it, adopting her part as helpless victim. "Oh! Thank god you're here!"

The police officer didn't seem to react to her act, though. "Natasha Markham, you're under arrest for the attempted murder and false imprisonment of Breanne Emmerson and for the false imprisonment and torture of Humphrey Black. You have the right to remain silent...."

Natasha couldn't believe what she was hearing. Her? Arrested? She was outside the law. Above it. She worked for the man who wrote the laws. They couldn't arrest her.

She heard the cuffs clink as they closed painfully around her wrists, snapping her out of her stupor. "You have the wrong person!" she protested. "Senator Lewitt! He's the one you should arrest! I was just following his orders!"

Epilogue

I broke the story on the news two days after the incident, and the scandal brought nationwide attention to the senator for days. Suzanne was shocked at my discoveries, but after finding Noah's body in the server rooms, her desire to run the story was doubled with a familiar need for justice.

Rumors of the senator running for the presidential office in a few years were quickly quashed. The man played a very good cleanup and backpedaling game, but the evidence we had gathered was too massive. More victims, from other cities around the state, stepped forward with their stories. While I doubted the validity of a few of them, a pattern of incidents like Liza's was clear. Liza's friend, Brian, was found dead of a gunshot wound, and ballistics matched the personal gun owned by the senator.

The senator's crimes had seen the light of day. I, for my part, felt glad to participate in exposing them. Justice would reign once again.

Even though I had told the organization originally that I would only be with them until I had seen the work with the senator come to a close, I knew now I would stay. These people were my closest friends, and had saved my life repeatedly throughout the incident.

Six months to the day after the incident on Plains Road, I had sat in the witness stand, reciting everything I could recall about those eventful few days. Several others had agreed to testify as well, though Saturday had declined in order to keep his identity secret.

With my, Black's, and the others' testimonies, combined with the footage I shot, the picture had become very clear to the jury. Markham had confessed, blaming the senator for everything.

Now, one week later, I sat in the back of the courtroom, waiting for the jury to return with their verdict. So much had changed.

The defense for Senator Lewitt had tried to scatter blame, even some on myself and Liza Strating, but Gold was as good at being a lawyer as Green was a fighter or Cyan an actor.

They helped bring meaning to what I did. To who I was. I was the white light, revealing to the world the darkest secrets of criminals who thought they were above the law.

The foreman of the jury stood.

"Have you, the jury, reached a decision?" the judge asked.

"We have, your honor."

"Proceed."

"We, the jury, find the defendant guilty on all charges."

Applause erupted in the room. I drank it in, glad for the verdict. It would not bring back Lucy, Noah, Brian, or the Silver twins, but the now-former senator would be put away for a long time.

Justice had been served.

www.ingramcontent.com/pod-product-compliance
Lightning Source LLC
Chambersburg PA
CBHW032119170626
46808CB00006B/2012